Tales from the Perseus Arm Volume II

I0659456

Edited by

Sam Taylor

Edited by Sam Taylor

ISBN Electronic Version: 978-0-9925415-2-1

ISBN Print Version: 978-0-9925415-3-8

Tales from the Perseus Arm
Volume II
(a science fiction anthology)

The international alliance of science fiction authors continues, comprising some award-winning authors, the cream of the upcoming crop of authors, and a couple of newly published authors whose work caught the eye of editor Sam Taylor. These writers were hand-picked from thousands of authors, from the US, UK, Ireland and Australia. Cover artist Patricia Burn returns with her characteristic stamp of brilliance.

Tales from the Perseus Arm (Volume II) is a collection of 14 original stories about robots, aliens, the depths of space, the astounding future and the sometimes troubling things that happen to the humans who have to cope with all of this. *Tales from the Perseus Arm* is fresh and original and will enchant both existing and new science fiction fans alike. We had enormous fun writing this, and we hope that you will have just as much fun reading it.

Edited by Sam Taylor

Table of Contents

Edited by Sam Taylor

INFLUENCE

By Kate Welty

Never without the White poised over
Sometimes seen, sometimes not,
But pulling always - now more, now less.
Water reveals it; tides moving
First this way, then that.

Were our natures built by that?
Obedient to its push and pull?
What need to battle was bred within
By never resting seas?

Suppose we travel far from the White
Out of that influence; no push nor pull.
Will our natures alter, be calmer?
More constant or more kind?
Less prone to restlessness and strife?

Or do we need strife?
Crave and create it
If it's gone too long?

Imagine other planets under other suns
No moon; no influence
No battle for survival
Within quiet, empty seas. No life?
Would we be boring, dull?

Oh Moon

What have you done to us?
For us?

Edited by Sam Taylor

WAVELENGTH

By Rachael Kelly

April 27th, 2047, NeuRIS testing laboratories, Saddler-Vanburen HQ, Project Leader Dr. Amy Moore supervising field testing of the Hermes project prototype g-force regulation suits, Mark 6.3. Also in attendance: Dr. Jonah Broekemeier, IASA, and Dr. Michael Fleiss, Saddler-Vanburen, laboratory assistant to Dr. Moore. Systems check shows green lights across the board, subject is prepped and ready to go, showing limited stress response; heart rate slightly elevated at 78 bpm, blood pressure at 134/85 compared to 115/75 resting. Adrenaline levels climbing, pain response is negligible. Starting the clock at 1543 hours, T minus 10 and counting.

00:00:04

T minus 6. Main engines firing. Heart rate +3 to 81bmp. Subject experiencing stress response well within normal limits. B/p remains normal. Pain measuring 0.3 als observed along with minimal tightening of chest as vibration intensity increases.

00:00:10

T minus 0. Liftoff.

00:00:18

Pain measuring 1.5 als and climbing. Acceleration at 1.8G. 1.9G. 2G. Pain measuring 1.7 als. B/p 154/90. Vitals good, adrenaline levels steady.

00:01:35

Pain levels constant at 1.1 als. Acceleration dropping to 1.5G. B/p steady at 150/90. Reading slightly reduced pulse ox and brain perfusion; synaptic responses remain good.

00:08:17

Acceleration increasing — 2.2G — 2.6G — 3.1G — and falling back to 2.9. Reading an increased pain output at 1.9 als and elevated heart rate at 90 bpm. Synaptic responses slightly reduced but well within range.

00:08:51

Acceleration constant at 3G. B/p at 164/90. Pain at 2.7 als with pronounced stress response. And... pain levels rapidly decreasing as acceleration drops to 2.5 — 2.0 — 1.0 — 0.5. I'm picking up a moderate vestibular response. Subject is experiencing mild nausea; no signs of disorientation, ocular response normal.

00:15:00

Maintaining steady speed at 27,000 mph. Subject continues to experience mild nausea. Heart rate 65 bpm. Blood pressure 120/75. Vitals good. Synaptic patterns good. Subject relaxed but alert.

00:20:00

Preparing to fire initial stage propulsion jets. Heart rate +3 and well within normal limits. G-force mitigation system coming online. Crosscheck shield integrity and perform initial fluid flush-through.

00:20:10

Shield integrity at 8.8 and rising. Viscous dampeners perfusing well. Heart rate steady at 65 bpm; mild discomfort as suit perfuses — registering at 0.7 to 0.8 als. Picking up a mild stress response but vitals are good. Respiratory rate slightly shallow — mild adrenal response detected, pulse ox good, synaptic function normal.

00:20:30

Shield integrity at 15.3 and holding. Full perfusion achieved. B/p 135/80, heart rate elevated but well within range. Firing initial stage propulsion jets.

00:20:30

Commencing initial acceleration at 60,000 miles per hour squared. Initial stage propulsion jets looking good. Subject's vitals are good, pain is steady at 0.5 als, heart rate steady, b/p steady. Shield integrity at 15.1 and holding. Looking good for phase two acceleration. Stand by to initialise Hermes system.

00:20:40

Hermes system online. Shield integrity at 15.1 and holding. Acceleration at 0.7G, climbing to 0.8 — subject comfortable at 0.3 als and steady. Stand by to launch Hermes propulsion system in T minus 5 — 4 — 3 — 2 — 1...

00:20:50

Hermes propulsion system is go. Shield integrity is at 15.2 and holding; acceleration is at 7.5G. 7.8G. 8.0. Heart rate is at 85 bpm and climbing; stress response rising. I'm reading a rapid adrenalin surge, b/p is climbing. Acceleration at 8.5G.

Suit perfusion is good, shields are at 15.2 and holding.

00:21:15

Heart rate at 90bpm. Acceleration at 9.3G. B/p at 168/95 and I'm reading 3.4 als and climbing. Suit perfusion is steady.

00:22:00

B/p steady. Suit perfusion good. Acceleration at 12.0G and climbing.

00:23:15

Acceleration at 15.0G. Subject experiencing respiratory discomfort and increasing O2 levels to compensate. Ocular responses normal; I'm reading fluctuating pain levels of between 3.7 and 4.5 als. B/p is 170/95.

00:24:37

Acceleration is at 17.0G, I'm seeing mild hypoxemia. Subject is increasing O2 to maximum. Shield integrity is good, suit perfusion is good. B/p at 168/95 and steady.

00:26:25

Acceleration at 22G. Shield integrity is stable at 15.3 and holding. Subject is experiencing moderate respiratory distress. Increasing suit perfusion to compensate. Motor function is… motor function is impaired, switching to automatic controls. Suit perfusion increasing. I don't like his — Mike, cross-check the algiometer; I don't like the readings I'm getting…

00:26:57

Acceleration at 25G and holding. Subject experiencing intermittent grey-outs, O2 sats dropping. Heart rate at 170

bpm and I'm reading 7.8 als at full perfusion — 8 als - 8.2...
Severe tachycardia, O2 sats are tanking, he's in trouble...

00:27:15

That's a full 10.0 on the algiometer. Pulse ox is 91% and falling. Severe respiratory distress. That's 10.1 — 10.2. 10.3 and still climbing...

00:27:27

Respiration has failed, initiating life support...

00:28:38

He's in VF. Charging to 260, preparing to... Asystole. Charging to 260... Defibrillator administered; subject remains asystolic. Charging to 300...

00:33:17

Subject non-responsive to therapeutic efforts. Neurological read-outs consistent with complete cessation of brainstem activity — diagnosis of brain death given by Dr. Moore, confirmed by Dr. Fleiss.

Mission terminated.

*

"*Damn* it!"

The words were softly spoken — Jonah's volume settings didn't generally go past a 7 — but they were fuelled by the kind of explosive frustration that could break a window. Amy released a soft puff of air, rolled the tension out of her shoulders, and turned to her assistant.

"All right, Mike," she said. "Run the systems analysis and buzz it to my data pocket when it's done. Dr. Broekemeier…" A glance towards the far end of the control pod, where Jonah stopped pacing just long enough to meet her eyes. "…let's go get some coffee."

She'd known him for a little over eight months, since he'd first approached Saddler-Vanburen with his proposal for their simulation suites, and she'd thought even then that he looked too old for his face. He was young — mid-thirties, she guessed — with the stoop shoulders and grey skin of a man who spends too much time hunched over a desk, and a dullness to his brown eyes that spoke of a prodigious intellect turned inwards. He wore no wedding band, but his hand drifted to his left ring finger when he was preoccupied, as though he'd once been accustomed to finding it less empty.

"Jonah," said Amy again, and his eyebrows arched, gaze dropping wearily to the floor.

"Yes," he said: one quiet syllable appended to the tail-end of a sigh. "Coffee. Thank you, Dr. Moore. Dr. Fleiss… I'd like to see that systems report too, when it's ready."

"No problem," said Mike, but he was half a second too late: Jonah's mind had already moved past him and on to other things.

She was expecting the question as soon as the control room door slid shut behind them, but he let the silence carry them three paces down the corridor before he spoke, which was probably a bad sign. Things got worse for Amy when

Jonah mulled them over.

"Are you sure…?" he said, but she was ready for him and cut him off while the sentence was still forming.

"Yes," she said, simply. "You know I am."

"I know you have confidence in your machines…"

"You do too," she told him. "It's why you're here."

"The suit stood up to *everything* we threw at it in the lab."

"And it doesn't stand up to NeuRIS." Amy pushed open the door to the break room, held it open for him to enter. "That's the same thing as a mid-deployment failure and you know it. Jonah, there's a reason you came to me — you need to know if your suit is going to do what it's designed to do before you put a actual human being in it and press a button, and hope none of IASA's best and brightest go and die a horrible death live on global television." She followed him into the room as he made his way over to the coffee dock, back turned to her, head bowed. "You have your answer," she said. "You just don't like it."

Jonah lifted a carafe of tepid Java from the burner, tilted it, sniffed at it suspiciously, as though he were trying to decide if it was worth the risk. Amy watched absently as he swirled it and poured, coffee splashing inelegantly into his mug, spilling up over the sides and pooling on the work-surface below.

"Hermes is scheduled to launch in less than 36 months," he said quietly. "I can't keep going back to the Project Board and telling them that eight years of R&D still hasn't managed to come up with a functional g-suit for the crew. There comes a point where they don't want to hear it anymore."

Amy shrugged, reached for the coffee. "Jonah, I don't know what to tell you," she said. "You can wait for the report if you like, but you know what it's going to say — catastrophic cardiovascular failure due to sustained high-g acceleration. *Again.* The suits do not work."

He sucked in a breath, half-turned away. "You know, maybe if you recalibrated..."

"Sure." Amy sipped from her mug. "Yeah, sure, Jonah, I'll recalibrate. And then I'll write it up in the procedurals, and *you* can explain to the grieving families why all fifteen astronauts died when the propulsion engines came online."

He shook his head. "Yes, all right."

"'Sorry, Mr and Mrs Parent. I guess we were just really, really hoping that the machines were wrong...'"

"I said all right." A rare grin tugged lopsidedly at one cheek, and Jonah's eyes slid sideways to meet hers. "You know, I can't decide sometimes if you're my conscience or my mother."

Amy grinned back. "Neither. I'm just doing my job."

"Yeah." A long sigh and his gaze drifted to the floor. "You know, I've just... I've got to go across town now and explain to a team of guys who don't speak science why we're back at square one again, and... you know. I'd just prefer not have to do that."

"It's not square one," said Amy, but Jonah shook his head.

"That's not how it looks in a board room," he said.

"We got up to 25G today. That's something. NeuRIS tanked at 18 last time."

"Yes." Jonah drained his cup, set it down on the counter, raised his hands to massage both temples. "But Hermes is designed to run at 40."

Amy shrugged. "It's something," she said. "We're only eight months into testing. I've seen projects stretch four times as long and still deliver."

"I don't have four times as long."

"No," she said, "But we're not out of time yet, either. Let's go reset the system and give it another shot."

*

It was dark by the time Amy shouldered open the door to her flat, arms overflowing with files, shopping bags and take-out sushi bought on impulse when her stomach realised abruptly just how long it had been since she'd last eaten. Her notepad had been buzzing for the past five floors of the elevator's ascent, but all but two of Amy's fingers were presently occupied with carrying things, and deploying the pair of them now would involve a fundamental and potentially disastrous reorganisation of her physiological make-up in order to answer a message that could almost certainly wait another fifteen seconds. It would be Mike, she thought, patching through the results of the systems crosscheck that Jonah had browbeaten them into running before he'd agree to leave for the day, and she already knew what it was going to say. So did Jonah, of course, but he wasn't the one who had to stay late to make it happen.

"All *right*," she muttered as she decanted two armfuls of groceries onto the kitchen counter. "I heard it; I'm not deaf. Re-route to the central cortex and place it in holding — I'll open it in a minute."

A flash of acknowledgement from the control strip on her wrist, and the buzzing stopped. Amy sucked in a deep breath and reached for the wine.

In a minute, she'd start the bath running, route today's analysis through to the bathroom, scroll through it while she sank into bubbles with a glass of burgundy in her hand: arcane lines of words and numbers, pulse oximetry readouts and source code, the computer-simulated annihilation of a human life. Once, when the NeuRIS project was young and Amy was the developer responsible for designing and maintaining a machine whose job it was to die a thousand deaths on demand, the lab reports had the power to keep her awake at night: radiation poisoning that cooked a person from the inside out; infant survival rates in low-ox, no-ox, full vacuum; compression injuries sustained at diving depths that would crumple reinforced steel — there was hardly a nightmare end that someone, somewhere, didn't want to explore in glorious technicolor. But almost twelve years behind the screen had silenced the shades of screams unvoiced, uncrunched buckled bones, and turned it all back into a steady stream of words and numbers on a VDU. The whole point of NeuRIS was that nobody died.

The wine was rich and ruby-red, spilling thick oak flavours into the air as it fell into the glass, staining the sides with liquid the colour of hypoxic blood. Amy lifted it to her lips, breathing deeply and closing her eyes, feeling fatigue wash through her and sing her brain into a comfortable lull. In a minute, she'd kick herself back into action, reboot and reanimate, start the evening's closing manoeuvres. In a minute. For now, there was wine and silence, slackening muscles, neurons powering down... and the tinny buzz of an incoming message from someone who clearly just could not take a hint.

"Goddamn it," she muttered, and raised a hand to pinch the bridge of her nose. "All *right*. Put it through. Yeah. This is Moore."

"Amy." Mike's voice, as expected. She wondered, briefly, if there were labour laws against firing someone for excessive enthusiasm in the performance of their duties. And then she glanced up at the display screen, hovering twelve inches in front of her face, and saw the look in his eyes.

"Mike," she said. "What is it? What's up?"

"I'm sorry to call so late..."

"Forget it." Amy shook her head, frustration forgotten as her brain belatedly registered the edge to his tone. "Is everything okay?"

"I think..." he said, and his voice wavered. "You need to get down here right away, Amy. There's... something's happened."

"What, Mike?" Impatience was creeping in. "What's

happened? What's going on?"

"Amy, it's NeuRIS," he said, and his eyes widened, as though he couldn't believe what he was about to say. "There's been an explosion."

"A *what?*"

"Amy… they're saying it's a bomb."

*

Saddler-Vanburen's headquarters occupied a purpose-built laboratory complex in the centre of a sprawling industrial park, where leafy avenues and wide, clipped-grass lawns painted over lines of steel and glass with a manufactured ideal of pastoral tranquility. On any given day, Amy could expect to pass no more than half a dozen cars on the drive that led to the geometric lines of the building's central plaza; this late at night, ordinarily, she'd have been surprised to have found anyone on the road but her. But tonight, even before she pulled up to the security gates that separated the folks that had cause to visit a multi-million dollar research centre from the folks that didn't, she could see that the distant lobby was alive with activity, cars crowded along the pavements and spilling police, fire crews, and journalists into the waiting arms of stone-faced security guards placed like breakwaters across the wide entrance.

"Jesus," she muttered under her breath, and pulled up on the verge.

Her security pass cleared a path for her through the worst excesses of hangers-on and carried her as far as the basement, where a uniformed sergeant met her as the elevator doors opened, and tried to turn her back. The scent of burning plastic hung heavily in the air, scattered by the constant motion of bodies moving along the corridor, and a few yards down the passageway, Amy could just see the edges of a blackened blast-scar staining the walls before it disappeared behind a curtain of forensic sheeting.

"I'm Amy Moore," she told the officer as he dodged her attempts to skirt around him. "I'm the Project Leader; this is my lab. I need to get through…"

"Amy!" Mike's voice, never so welcome. She glanced up in the direction of his shout, pitched from the opposite direction to her shattered laboratory, and found him shrouded in a blue paramedic's blanket, leaning heavily against the frame of the break room's open door. With a lurch of guilt, Amy realised that it had never occurred to her to ask if he was all right: her first thought had been for NeuRIS. She wondered now just how close he'd been to the explosion.

"Mike!" she said. "Christ. Are you okay?"

One hand gripped the corners of the blanket together at his throat, the other reached out to take her shoulder, guiding her away from the cordon and the chaos towards the relative quiet of the coffee dock. Even through the fabric of her spring coat, the suit jacket and blouse beneath it, she could feel the tremor in his fingers. "I'm okay," he said. "I was in the control room at the time. I'm not hurt."

"You're shaking."

"Yeah, well, I was just in an explosion."

The break room served the east corridor of the lower labs; twenty to twenty-five people on a busy day. Tonight, three of the six tables were occupied: scatterings of uniforms, the rudiments of a triage kit, three scientists from the PHPL project down the hallway, and a party of suits who looked like they might represent the upper echelons of management, sipping coffee and talking in low tones. Amy wasn't sure she liked the look of that.

"Jesus," she said in a low tone, eyes fixed on the group in the far corner as she pulled out a chair for her assistant. "Mike, what the hell happened here tonight?"

"Damned if I know," he said as he sat. "I was just sitting at my console, finishing up with Jonah's reports, next thing I know, I'm on the ground and the room's full of smoke. Amy, I didn't see anything, I didn't hear anything — I didn't even know it was a bomb until the police showed up."

"You're sure you're okay?"

"Rattled," he said, and flashed a half-smile that almost met his eyes. "That's all. They checked me over, I swear."

"You want some coffee? I'll get you some coffee."

"God, no. I've got so much adrenalin pumping through my veins I think my heart might actually quit if I top it up with caffeine. I'm fine, Amy. I promise."

"Would you tell me if you weren't?"

"Well, I'm going to let you talk me into taking three days'

paid recuperation leave, put it that way."

Despite herself, Amy grinned. "Hey, it's not like there's going to be much work for you, the rest of the week." And then, as quickly as it came, the smile was gone, and she felt the blood drain from her face, her eyes fill with tears. "Jesus, Mike. My machines. All those years of work…"

"Hey," he said softly, and one shaking hand stretched out across the table to grip hers. "We'll be fine, Amy. It's not as bad as it looks, I swear."

"Mike, there's a forensics team crawling all over the blast-charred fragments of my mainframe right now…"

"The mainframe wasn't hit."

"They've sealed off the whole corridor…!"

"Yeah, the lab's pretty messed up, don't get me wrong. But the mainframe's intact, Amy. The damage was limited to the storage pods."

"The *storage* pods?" Amy had never thought of herself as the sort of person that defaulted into repetition in a moment of crisis, but, then again, she felt, the circumstances were extenuating. "But… That's just historical data. Why would anyone want to blow it up?"

Mike shrugged. "You're asking the guy whose ears are still ringing from a blast concussion," he said. "Talk to the DCI in charge of the investigation — Coren, I think he said his name was. He has a bunch of questions for you anyway. Word to the wise: the man has no sense of humour. I think I just got my name added to some kind of list."

"Where is he now?"

"Talking to Janowicz. They've commandeered the CyGen offices for interviews. I'm guessing someone'll come and get you when they're ready."

"Okay," said Amy. "And then I'm driving you home."

Inexplicably, Mike grinned, shook his head. "Maybe talk to Coren first," he said. "But, yeah, that sounds good to me."

*

The reason for his amusement became clear somewhere around hour three of sitting around and doing nothing, but it was another two and a half before Amy was called into Coren's impromptu command centre to speculate on the identity of two faces caught on camera in the storage pods eighteen minutes before an explosion left a smoking crater where twelve years worth of data used to be. But Mike was right: they had back-ups, they had insurance, and they had the central processing mainframe. NeuRIS would live to fight another day.

It was closing in on 3:30 am when she pulled up in front of Mike's apartment block, a muted glow behind the curtains of his third floor window testifying to Andrew's wakefulness in his partner's absence. The tremors had finally quit about an hour into their sojourn in the break room, but, as the adrenal tide had receded, the shadows beneath Mike's eyes had deepened, his shoulders had slackened, his skin had lost its colour, until he looked as though he might be knocked off his feet by a well-aimed sneeze. Another fifteen minutes, Amy thought, and he'd have passed out face-down on the table.

"Go get some sleep," she told him as he scrubbed fists into the balls of his eyes, as though he were trying to rub enough life back into his brain to get him out of the car and into his flat. "No sense in coming in tomorrow. I'll let you know when we can get back into the lab."

Mike nodded, but he made no move to open the passenger door. "You gonna be okay, boss?" he asked.

"Me?" said Amy. "I'm not the one just watched us get blown into next week."

"You know what I mean."

Amy laughed, low and humourless. "I'll be fine."

"What are you going to do?"

"Right now, I'm going home to run a bath and drink about a quart of wine."

"Tomorrow."

"Tomorrow, I'm going to sleep off all the wine I'm going to drink tonight," said Amy. "Seriously, Mike — don't worry about me. NeuRIS is going to be fine; I'm going to be fine. I guess I'll just put my feet up for a day or two and try not to answer any of Jonah's calls until I know how long my damn machines are going to be offline."

A wide grin stripped a little of the fatigue out of Mike's face. "Good luck with that."

"Yeah, I'm giving him twenty-four hours and then I'm telling him to call you."

"I'm ex-directory."

"I'll give him your number."

"I'll change my number."

She laughed, punched him affectionately on the shoulder. "Get out of my car before you collapse and I have to carry you up three flights of stairs."

"I gotta say," he said, as the door swung open and cool, late-spring air rushed into the car, "I think I like your chances of that better than your chances of keeping Jonah off your back." Mike stepped out onto the pavement, leaned his head back through the door. "Let me know if there's anything I can do to help, okay?"

"Sure," said Amy. "I'll see you in a few days."

*

The fact was, she thought, as the garage doors trundled open onto the depths of the car park, that she had no answers for Jonah, Coren, Saddler-Vanburen, or the half-dozen journalists that had pressed her for a quote as she and Mike made their way through the same security gates that had conspicuously failed to prevent a pair of bombers sneaking explosives into her lab a few hours earlier. NeuRIS' clients came from across the world — governments and capital investment firms, international conglomerates and private companies; anyone with money to spare and a vested interest in determining human tolerances to the sort of things you weren't allowed to trial in person — but, while the projects were occasionally controversial and sometimes ethically questionable, there was nothing in the storage pods that Amy could imagine causing problems for anyone if it fell into the wrong hands. Some of it was classified, all of it was subject to a series of iron-clad non-disclosure agreements, but that was as much about protecting Saddler-Vanburen's intellectual property as it was about the content of the documents in question. Maybe somebody, somewhere, would be embarrassed to have the world find out that he'd asked NeuRIS to determine the morbidity of autoerotic asphyxiation in a low-oxygen environment, but, given that no one was ever likely to question or even care what secrets Amy's mainframe could tell, she couldn't imagine the circumstances under which a person might be prepared to risk jail time to silence them for good.

She was tired. She was tired, and she was shaken and, no matter how limited the damage might be, she was worried about her machines. Right now, what she needed was sleep, and sleep was almost certainly not going to happen, and the thought of lying wakeful, pillow pulled over her face while the skies lightened and the small hours grew long and a thousand restless thoughts danced allegro around the inside of her skull, made her head ache. Amy pulled her car to a stop in her parking space and sat back heavily in her seat, breathing deeply, eyes closing of their own accord in the quiet half-light of the underground lot. Maybe she could just stay here, snatch a few hours' unconsciousness while her hyperactive neurons weren't paying attention, wake up to darkness when she was ready and then work out where to go from there...

And so it was that Amy neither heard nor saw the man approaching her car until he was level with the driver's side window, with a gun pointed directly at her face.

At first, she wasn't certain what she was seeing. Rather, she *was*, but the night had already delivered her one bomb, and Amy was just not the sort of person to whom violent things happened; there was a part of her brain that was hard-wired to find it more probable that she'd fallen asleep without noticing than that her car was actually being hi-jacked. But then he waved the gun and the dim overhead light caught on the barrel — a bright flash of starlight in the gloom — and something about the gesture, soft and strangely poetic, cut through the comfortable shell of denial, set her heart racing, trapped her breath in her chest. There was a man with a gun at her window. And he was pointing it at Amy's face.

"Don't move," he said. "Hands on the steering wheel — slowly. Reach for the horn and you're dead."

"Okay, sure," she said, and she could hear the panic in her voice, clipping each syllable. "Take the car. The keys are in the ignition."

He was small, narrow-built, with a hooded jacket pulled tight around his face and obscuring his features, but he moved like a young man — Amy guessed late teens or early twenties. Wiry, but he carried himself easily, gracefully, like a man trained for combat. Even if he hadn't had the advantage, Amy wasn't sure she could have fought him off.

"Yeah, I'll take the car," he said, gun fixed, motionless, on her temple. "But you're coming too, Dr. Moore."

*

There were things you were supposed to do. She knew there were. Attract attention, flash the headlights, drive into a wall; anything to let the world outside the car know that things were not okay within. But it turned out that all of those things looked a hell of a lot more reckless when there was a man in the passenger seat with a loaded weapon trained on your hip and an encyclopaedic knowledge of which city streets would be least occupied at this time of night. Amy tried talking to him, asking where they were going, how he knew her name, why he'd taken her, but the man spoke only to give directions and, out of the city, he made her pull over, put a canvas bag over her head, tied her wrists and ankles, and pushed her into the boot. Amy was beyond fear. She had no idea what to do next.

So instead she made herself run through lines of code, histopathological readouts, the digital science of a human heart; anything that focused her brain away from what was happening. Her clothes still smelled of smoke and burned plastic; her fingers were turning numb from the cords that closed over her radial pulse; she could taste blood at the back of her mouth as rapid breaths scraped over a throat parched by panic. Seven hours ago, she'd been opening a bottle of wine and expecting nothing more exciting from her evening than lavender-scented bubbles and a lengthy systems report;

now she was bound and gagged in the back of her own car, driving to who knew where, with an explosion in her immediate past and a man with a gun in her present. Amy ran through typical causes of metabolic acidosis, learned years ago for a high-profile crush-injury simulation, and tried not to wonder what that promised for her future.

She had no idea how far they'd driven when she felt the car pull onto rougher ground, slow to a crawl, and then stop, but the air that rushed into the boot as the bonnet swung open was clean and fresh, and the first hints of dawn filtered through the burlap that covered her face. Rough hands grabbed her beneath her arms and pulled her upright, and, involuntarily, Amy cried out as stiff muscles protested the sudden movement. Nobody made any reply.

They left the bindings on her hands and legs and half-carried, half-dragged her between two thick-set, solid bodies that she categorised as male on the basis of their height and demonstrable upper body strength. The light outside her blindfold darkened as Amy's feet scraped over a threshold, and she felt herself hauled across an uneven wood flooring, scents of damp and mould flavouring the air: the odour of neglect, of abandonment, of a lonely place where nobody would think to look for a woman whose absence would go unnoticed for several days at least. A couple of long-legged strides carried them forwards perhaps three or four feet, before the men drew to a halt as the sound of a turning lock rattled in the quiet air, and a door creaked open in front of them. Clammy darkness spilled over Amy, and then the men were lifting her, raising her almost completely off the ground like a sack of sand. Her shoulder joints shrieked again, sucking the breath from her lungs, but before she could adjust, she was moving downwards, bones thudding against muscle as she was carried down a set of steps and planted firmly on a solid stone floor. The air was cool and moist, stale with disuse, but the ground felt dry as Amy's feet shuffled across it, and she thought she caught a trace of ozone through the canvas, as though high-voltage electronics were running nearby. That wasn't exactly a comforting thought, and the snap of cuffs around her wrists, the tinny rattle as they connected with something solid and metallic fixed to a rough-plastered wall, didn't particularly help.

The hands released her; Amy felt the men withdraw, felt the shift in the micro-currents of the basement air that told her that, in this small corner of the room, she was alone. Instinctively, she tugged at her restraints, felt them connect with whatever held her in place, felt the bite of steel against flesh.

"Please," she whispered. "Please, someone just tell me why I'm here. I'll give you whatever you want. Please. I'm just a programmer; I'm not important. *Please.*"

"Just a programmer." The voice was low, bitter, and completely unexpected. Amy felt her breath catch in her throat, her footing almost fail as she spun in place to seek out its source. "You're a sadist, is what you are, Dr. Moore." A woman — soft-spoken with fury, standing about fifteen feet away. "You're sick, is what you are. What you do is obscene."

"Please!" cried Amy, and she could hear desperation frosting the edge of her voice. "You've made a mistake, I swear! I write computer code, that's all I do! I don't know what you want!"

"That's why you're here," said the voice quietly. "You and I are going to have a chat about how you like to torture things, Amy. And then you're going to go back to Saddler-Vanburen and shut your project down."

*

There were five of them. At least, there were five separate sets of footfalls on the basement floor: the two heavy-set men who'd carried her from the car; the soft-spoken woman; another woman whose shoes had a nail or a piece of gravel caught in one sole that clicked against the floor as she walked; and a fifth person, light on their feet, who didn't speak but who might have been the man who'd brought her here. Soft-Spoken Fury sat on a chair on the other side of the room, its wooden legs rasping against the concrete when she moved, and exchanged brief words with Click-Shoe as she clipped back and forward. Sometimes, there would be a burst of static from a far corner; sometimes a clattering of keyboards and a faint hum on the very edge of hearing; and once Amy heard a muttered reference to acetone peroxide that elicited a flurry of excitable whispers and a *fucking stupid idiots* from a male voice that she didn't recognise. They gave her water after a couple of hours, rolling up the burlap blindfold just enough to expose her mouth, and she drank it carefully: just enough to wet her throat and hold off dehydration for a little longer. Amy didn't want to think about what happened if she needed to pee.

"Two point seven hours post-exposure," said Soft-Spoken Fury from her floor-scraping seat as the canvas was rolled back down and re-fastened at Amy's throat. She'd been reading from NeuRIS systems records for over three-quarters of an hour now, and no amount of protest could make her stop, though it could garner threats of actual bodily harm from Heavies One and Two that sounded genuine enough that Amy didn't feel inclined to test their commitment. "Headache now registering at 6.44 als. Vomiting largely non-responsive to anti-emetics; electrolyte balance currently maintained through delivery of IV fluid replacement. Synaptic responses generally poor; subject experiencing intermittent loss of consciousness and periods of extreme disorientation.

"Three point three hours post-exposure. Generalised, systemic pain registering between 7.8 and 8.0 als, reducing to 6.7 on maximum anaesthesia. Blood observed in vomitus. Ventricular arrhythmia now pronounced despite increasing IV potassium to 10 mEq/l/hr.

"Four hours post-exposure. Following a latent period of approximately 1 hour, subject has experienced a rapid recurrence and escalation of symptoms. CNS syndrome now advanced, with severe ataxia and cognitive impairment. Pain registering 8.7 als with no further anaesthesia possible..."

"I remember," said Amy, who knew what was coming next and didn't feel inclined to relive it. "I remember all of them."

"No you don't," said Soft-Spoken Fury. It was the first thing she'd said in almost an hour that wasn't Amy's own words from years gone by. "You remember notes on a page.

You remember lines of code. You don't remember the suffering."

"What suffering." It wasn't a question; it was barely even a statement, breathed out on the end of a wave of fatigue so absolute that Amy wasn't sure she could have held her head up without a wall to support it. "There is no suffering. For God's sake, I *prevent* suffering. That simulation, that was a control study for a drug designed to reverse Acute Radiation Sickness. It saved lives."

"At what cost, Amy?"

"You want me to run NeuRIS for free? Is that it?"

"This isn't about money and you know it."

"Then what? *What?*" One Herculean act of will pulled her into a sitting position, spine straightening, knees closing in on her chest. "I don't know what you want. I don't know what you want me to say!"

"March 7th, 2040..."

"For God's sake! I know what the reports say! I wrote the reports!"

"Then tell me, Amy." Wood scraped concrete and a single, soft footfall described a body rising to stand but moving no closer. "What kind of a sociopath writes page after page after page describing the worst kind of agony — what kind of sociopath lists pain measurements like they're reading out the weather forecast, and then asks *what suffering* as though it's an exercise in the abstract? As though the whole point of the procedure isn't exactly about finding out just how much suffering a human body can take before it shuts down?"

"What are you talking about?" Frustration edged Amy's voice, making her reckless. "It's a machine! I wrote the damn code myself!"

"You built a brain that you could torture to death over and over again." The words were quiet, but there was an shade of menace to them that coloured them with shades of the zealot. "The only reason you get to sleep at night is because you didn't build it a mouth that it could use to scream. Someone has to be its voice. Someone has to speak for it."

"You blew up my lab," said Amy quietly. It didn't seem like an untenable leap to make, and there was no denial from the woman in the chair. "How does that give NeuRIS a voice?"

"We'll get to the mainframe eventually," said Soft-Voiced Fury. "No matter what happens, we're going to shut it down. For now, we stopped you hurting it for a little while and we wiped out its memory so it doesn't have to live with what you've done."

"It can't..." said Amy, but stopped herself before the words could finish forming. She had no idea what to say; no idea what might push her companion back into the realms of the rational, or what might earn Amy a bullet in the back of her head. Her best defence, she thought —for now at least — was silence.

There was a long pause, punctuated by clicks from the corner, the sub-sonic whisper of electronics. Amy could feel

Fury's eyes on her from across the room: an evaluative gaze or a murderous glare, she couldn't tell, and nothing she could do would stack the odds back in her favour. And then there was a quiet intake of breath in the still, hushed air, and a low, level voice began reading.

"March 7th, 2040. NeuRIS testing laboratories, Project Leader Dr. Amy Moore supervising. Also in attendance: Mark Buchanan and Professor Marie-Claude Anctil of the OEA, and Dr. Michael Fleiss, Saddler-Vanburen..."

Four hours one Wednesday afternoon almost a decade ago; a day too ordinary to live on in memory beyond a few perfunctory notes scrawled on a screen. Unseen beneath her canvas mask, Amy closed her eyes and leaned her head backwards to rest against the damp-plastered wall.

*

She must have slept, though she had no idea how long she'd been out; only that, when she opened her eyes again, it was to a fuzzy head and a dry mouth and the sensation of missing time. Soft-Voiced Fury had stopped speaking, but there was a low buzz of industry to the room: air currents gliding in the darkness, quiet footfall, murmured voices. Amy's arms had slid above her head as she'd slumped, fixed in place against the metal bar to which she was cuffed, and her fingers felt swollen, dead and bloodless where her veins had been constricted as she slept. She shuffled backwards, shackles rattling against their restraint, too loud in the hush, and she heard the room settle abruptly, as though it were holding its breath. Then one set of footsteps peeled off from the rest, and Amy heard them moving towards her, distinctive clip marking the owner's identity even before she crouched down in front of Amy to speak.

"Here," said Click-Shoe. "Water. Take a drink."

Amy's throat was so parched that it hurt to swallow, let alone speak, but she shook her head just the same. But her hands were tied and Click-Shoe's were not, which put one of them in definitive control of the situation, and, since Click-Shoe intended to administer fluids, fluids were going to be administered. Amy felt gentle fingers at the knot at her neck, loosening the binding; the rush of air on her chin, her cheeks, as the canvas was rolled up as high as her mouth and a canteen was pressed to her lips.

"Drink," said Click-Shoe. "You must be thirsty."

She was, and her body knew what it needed even if her brain preferred to occupy some kind of arbitrary high ground where dehydration was a sign of superior moral fibre. Amy leaned into the bottle as Click-Shoe tilted it to her mouth, water spilling down her chin and onto her chest as she drank, and, when it pulled away, her head followed it instinctively, mouth gaping open and dripping like a baby seeking milk.

"That's enough for now," said Click-Shoe. "You'll make yourself sick, Amy."

Amy sank back against the wall, catching her breath. "Why would you even care?" she asked.

"Because I'm the one who'd have to clean it up," said

Click-Shoe. "These other guys would let you sit in your own puke, you know."

Despite herself, tears pricked at Amy's eyes. "I haven't done anything," she whispered, and she could hear her voice shaking. "I don't know why I'm here. I don't know what you want."

"Yeah," said Click-Shoe, but her voice was kind. "You do. You just don't know that you know just yet. But, Amy, unless you start listening, we're going to have to show you. And I know you don't want that."

"What do you mean? Please — please don't hurt me..."

"I don't want to hurt you, Amy. I just want you to understand."

"I'm trying!" It was almost a wail: the sound of a child in distress, but there was nothing she could do to moderate the panic now. "I swear I am, I'm trying, but I just don't know what you want me to say!"

"Amy." Gentle patience. Amy wanted to trust that voice; she wanted to make that voice look after her. "Do you understand what NeuRIS is? Do you really understand it?"

"It's a programme, it's a computer programme." The words tumbled out of her, and, despite Click-Shoe's precautions, Amy could feel her stomach roiling mutinously. "It's designed to test the limits of human tolerances. It's designed to run simulations for clients who need to know how to keep people safe. That's all it is, I swear. It's supposed to keep people safe. The whole point of NeuRIS is that nobody dies."

"NeuRIS dies, though," said Click-Shoe softly. "Doesn't it?"

"No! You just... you can't... It can't die! It's a machine, it's lines of code. It's just a simulation; that's all it is. It tells us when we've exceeded physiological limits and it closes the programme. That's it! It's not conscious. It's not *alive*. It's a machine!"

"A machine designed to suffer."

"It can't suffer! It's not alive!"

"Okay, Amy. Tell me how NeuRIS works. Explain it like you're talking to a child."

"You know how it works..."

"Yes, I do. But I want to know if *you* know."

"I built it. I know how it works."

"Amy." A warning note, buried beneath layers of kindness, but sharp as frost. "I'm asking you to tell me."

"From... where? From the beginning?"

"From the beginning. A client approaches you..."

"A client approaches me." This was easy. Amy had explained this many times; her mouth knew the script without reference to her brain. "They tell us their hypothesis. I give them a questionnaire that they need to fill in: all the variables, all the questions they need to answer. I get as much detail as they can give me: what scenarios they need to look at, what age range they need to test, how healthy, how unhealthy the subject needs to be. The initial report can run to eighty, ninety pages sometimes. It has to be detailed or else they don't get the results they need."

"So you've got the details. What happens next?"

"My assistant, Mike — he draws up a preliminary schematic. I have a group of consultants that I use, physicians who know the programme, and I take them the prelims for feedback. There'll be a series of charts, data clusters that I need them to populate; I need them to sit in on the initial sim and make sure that NeuRIS is reacting the way they'd expect a human body to react. I need them to cross check the synaptic readouts, the biochemical interactions, the ECGs, the neural feedback relays — I need them to tell me if my sim is fit-for-purpose."

"You need them to tell you if NeuRIS is going to die when it ought to."

"I need them to tell me if the tolerances are correct. I can't take the chance that a sim might tell us a person could survive for 30 minutes if they could only survive for 29. I need to know that my code is robust."

"And how long does the consultation period last?"

"It depends…"

"On what?"

"Something we know a lot about — like food poisoning, maybe, or crush injuries — that might only take a couple of weeks. Something more complicated — we have to code for potentials, for inferred data, and it takes months to refine."

"And when does the pain signal go online?"

"That's part of the neural feedback relay…"

"I know what it is," said Click-Shoe. "I'm asking when it goes online."

"It changes," said Amy. "Sometimes, the pain signal is integral to the simulation, so we have to code for it from the very beginning. Sometimes it's part of the overall precision settings but non-essential, and we can let it slide for a little longer."

"But it's never absent."

"It can't be absent. Pain is intrinsic to human survival — I can't code for a simulation without factoring in critical avoidance strategies and the preservation reflex. We're too complex — any sim that ignored the role of pain in the progression of human injury would be useless. The results would be useless."

"Because you need to know *exactly* how a real-life human would react under the circumstances."

"Yes! If NeuRIS can't mimic human behaviour precisely, it's pointless. It might as well be guesswork."

"So it's a virtual human?"

"It's lines of code in a mainframe."

"Designed to respond exactly the way a human being would respond."

"That's right."

"And what, exactly, makes that different from a virtual human?"

"It doesn't have corporeal form. It doesn't... it's not sentient. It can't think."

"But it has a central nervous system…"

"It doesn't…"

"A *virtual* central nervous system."

"No!" Amy could hear her voice rising; struggled to control it. "It has lines of code that predict how a central nervous system would react."

"Okay." Click-Shoe's voice was calm, level. "And it does this by intercepting stimuli, interpreting them, and outputting the data as pain signals, right?"

"Yes. It interprets signals and outputs them as measurable data. That's all it does."

"Amy," said a voice, and it took her a second to understand that it belonged, not to Click-Shoe, but to the man who'd pulled the gun on her in the car park. "How is that different from what your central nervous system does?"

What could she say? How could she possibly explain the thousand ways they'd got it all wrong without defaulting to a blunt, inelegant, *because it just is*? Where were the words that explained that, though qubits and probability distributions might be made to look like nociceptors and parasympathetic motor functions, they were smoke and mirrors, a best guess refined to the point of virtual certainty, but meaningless without a mainframe to decode them? How could she convince five people who'd already convinced themselves?

And now there was a bustle of activity around her, and Amy felt hands tugging at her sleeves, the skin of her arms contracting as the fabric receded, exposing her flesh to the chilly air.

"What are you doing?" she asked, panic clouding her words and stealing her breath. "Don't — please, don't…"

"I told you," said Click-Shoe, and her voice was soft, almost sad. "I don't want to hurt you, but I need you to understand."

"Oh Christ!" Metal teeth, sharp and vicious, pinched and gripped the soft skin of Amy's forearm. "What are you doing? Please, God, please don't…"

"We're online," said a voice — female again, but different; a voice Amy didn't recognise. "I'm calling up the patterns now."

"Algiometer is go," said the Gun Man from a corner of the room, and Amy felt her legs buckle, cuffs biting into her wrists as she twisted and heaved at her restraints.

"Hold her down," said Click-Shoe, and Amy felt strong hands force her to the ground, the flash-chill of water pouring over her arms, soaking into her legs, her lap, her chest. "Amy. *Amy*. Listen to me. Listen. This is going to be over very quickly, but it has to happen. I need you to understand." And then, to someone beside her: "13,000 volts. Guys, let her go and stand back."

"No….!" screamed Amy, but the word died mid-breath as the current surged. The world went white.

*

"…read-outs? She's fine, leave her. I said, she's *fine*. I

know what I'm doing."

Distant voices, as though the speakers were underwater or far below the ground. Consciousness crept in, edged in black and frosted with pain, and Amy was dimly aware that she was stretched against the floor, arms suspended high above her head, body prostrated. Everything hurt. She wished she could pass out again.

A pinch at either arms, and a little pressure receded. It took her a moment to work out that the metal teeth had been bulldog clips, attached to some kind of electronic device, and that they were gone now, and that this might mean that the pain was finished. Her face was damp, but it was only when she heard the first sob that she realised she was crying.

"Sit up. Breathe, Amy." The Gun Man, close by her left ear. She wondered if he'd owned the hands that held her down. "It's over now. Take a minute, get your breath. I need you with me for this."

"Fuck you." The words tumbled out in a wash of tears and mucus; she hadn't realised she was going to say them until they were spoken. But they felt right; they felt good. "Fuck you," she said again. "Fuck all of you. Fuck you all to hell."

"See?" Click-Shoe's voice, unconcerned. "I told you she was fine. How are the read-outs looking?"

"Just about ready." Soft-Voiced Fury, significantly less furious; somewhere close by and to the left. "Okay — get her head. Everyone else, get out of sight. Let's do this."

Strong, thick fingers closed around the base of Amy's

skull, but, before she could cry out, make any noise of protest, the sack was pulled sharply upwards, over her head. Dim basement light flooded Amy's unaccustomed eyes and she blinked back tears as the world swam into focus, resolved into the shimmering pattern of a computer screen, inches from her face. Black on black, with a single red line streaking across the page and spiking in a chaotic profusion of electronic teeth that dropped, abruptly, into nothingness. Amy's brain was reeling from the current and the adrenaline, but it took her no more than a second to recognise what she was seeing.

An algiometric readout. The story of her own pain, scribbled across a screen.

"Fuck you," she said again, but her voice was full of tears.

"This is you," said Click-Shoe quietly. "This is what it looks like when someone tortures a human being. This is what the algiometer reads when the pain signal spikes. You couldn't scream because you had no voice, but your body knew how to tell the story. Amy — listen to me. This is what suffering looks like. And this..." A click, and then a line in green, mirror of the first, snaked across the page, following the troughs and peaks like the caress of a lover. "...This is one of 88 pain signals recorded on July 13th, 2046, during field tests of a electroshock weapon designed for large-scale use in riot-control. You remember that one, Amy? NeuRIS decided it was too dangerous for public deployment when six weeks of testing resulted in 472 death scenarios. And each one of them looked just like this."

"No..." But the word was thick, obscured by tears. "It's

not the same. It has to look like that; that's what it's supposed to look like…"

"Bullshit, Amy." The Gun Man again, but there was no violence in his voice. "It looks like that because it's pain. It's real pain, Amy. That's how you designed it. NeuRIS responds to the pain stimulus exactly the same way that a human being does — that you do — because that's what you need it to do. That's the only way you get results. The only difference is, it can't tell you what's happening. It can't tell you to stop."

"It's a machine."

"Yes. It is. It's a machine built specifically to hurt."

"Oh my God." Tears flowed freely; there was nothing she could do to stop them. "I didn't mean to. I swear… I didn't mean to."

"I know you didn't," said Click-Shoe now. "We know you didn't. But we can't let it continue either."

"Please," whispered Amy. "Please don't kill me."

"No." A flick of the wrist and the sack descended again, darkness flooding in around the memory of two lines on a screen. "If we wanted to kill you, we'd have killed you, Amy. That's not why you're here. You're here because we needed to make you understand. You can fix this, you can take the project apart and make sure it doesn't get rebuilt. But you can't do that if you're dead."

"You're going to…?" The unspoken thought hovered on the edge of hope, as though voicing it might make it disappear. "You're going to let me go?"

"Yes," said the Gun Man quietly. "We're going to let you go."

*

It was two days before the medical staff would allow DCI Coren into Amy's private ward, and, though she suspected that her injuries weren't serious enough to warrant the precaution, she was glad of it just the same. It gave her space to straighten things out in her head before she had to try and explain them to someone else.

"They called themselves Breath of Life," she told him as he stood at the foot of her bed, scribbling notes with a biro on old-fashioned paper notepad. He'd offered one of his rare smiles when she asked him about it; said he preferred a medium that nobody could hack. "I think they think they're some kind of rights movement for electronic intelligence. Vigilantes, or something."

"The auric signatures on your clothing are a match for DNA recovered from the blast scene," he told her. "We're closing in on them."

"Good," said Amy. The burns to her forearms were minor, concealed behind two neat gel patches, but they ached when she moved. "I'll sleep a lot better once I know they're behind bars."

"I don't think you have anything to worry about, Dr. Moore," said the inspector, with a nod of his head that was presumably supposed to be reassuring. "They set you free of their own accord. I doubt you'll be seeing them again."

Coren's was the sort of gruff, cheerless demeanour that encouraged a sense of security and confidence, from the sort of man that garnered trust without any kind of conscious effort, and his words were designed to put her mind at rest. But, Amy couldn't help but notice, he kept an officer stationed outside her door when he left.

Alone in her room, Amy called up the computer screen she'd been working at when he'd arrived, leaning back against her pillows as it unzipped out of the air in front of her: a single, serpentine green line against a sea of black. One hand, wrist bruised and welted from thirty-six hours spent chained to a length of piping, reached up to trace an imaginary twin just below the spikes and pits, her mind colouring it in shades of blood.

It had been almost an exact match: a silent scream of neurons, a song of suffering composed in shimmering pixels, misery mapped and transcribed for dispassionate eyes. Beat for beat, pulse for pulse, an echo of the code that Amy had written.

She'd have to get Mike to recalibrate, once the machines were back online. NeuRIS had been running lethal-dose sims; if they were peaking at the same al-frequency as a non-lethal voltage, then that meant that the alignments were off. But, then again, all things considered, she supposed it counted as useful feedback. There was no point in a sim that predicted a 30-minute survival window if it was actually more like 45.

One soft command closed the readout screen and Amy called up a message to Jonah, half-composed in the hours before she'd been taken away by a man with a gun; now ready to be populated with a definitive timescale for getting the Hermes field tests back up and running. If she could get Mike to run the new algiometer balances as part of the refit, then another week — ten days at most — would see them back in the labs, mainframe firing, cortex online, algiometrics refined, enhanced, and coded against real-time observations, more precise than ever before. It was good work. It was important work. It was testing the limits of human tolerance to make sure that human lives were saved.

After all, the whole point of NeuRIS was that nobody died.

Edited by Sam Taylor

LITTLE GHOST OF ELVIS

By Salvatore Barbie Lombard

He left his body worn and bloody-footed in the cave. He paused, just for a moment, to look back at it. There were bones thrusting from the bare back and scars creasing the shoulders. Sand dusted the face, punctuated by trailing sweat. The mouth hung slightly open. The expression was listless and exhausted.

I don't have long, he reflected.

If he was within an hour of the ship, he might make it. If not...

He reached the lip of the cave and looked out. The dunes rose high all around. Practically mountains of sand, they cast deep shadows. He surveyed those shadows for a sign of the Clearians. He saw nothing, but that didn't mean they weren't around. It meant only that they were cautious.

He lifted off and floated away. He left his body behind in the heat.

There was no life in the desert. This was far from the glimmering city of the Clearians, full of flowers and exotic pets. Rock formations loomed as the most interesting features of the land. Once he thought he saw the shadow of a bird, but it proved only to be a streak of black stone.

He saw none of the markers from his landing. He circled wider and wider, higher, until the dunes shrank to anthills below him.

Far removed from his body, he didn't panic.

Instead, he only wondered faintly; if his body died, what would happen to the rest of him?

He began to sink.

He couldn't feel the sunlight passing through him, but he remembered the pressing heat of his trek, and knew the temperature was only rising. Even the Clearians stayed indoors at the peak of day, extended their frills, and pumped the cold air.

What if his body had already died in his absence? Would he even feel it? Have felt it?

Oh god, he realized suddenly. What if I never get to eat another cheeseburger?

He dropped quickly, reaching the ground in a blip of a moment, and zoomed over the sand towards the cave where his body lay. He would check in, wake up, and make sure it wasn't dying yet. Then he would make another sweep.

A huge outcropping grew up on his right. It was pocked with great holes, like vesicular rock formed by an ancient, gargantuan volcano. As he zoomed along and it rose alongside, the sun fell away behind. The shadow passed over him. He glanced to his right. Something stirred. His flight stuttered as he turned to look.

And he came to a complete, screeching halt as something seized him around the waist. The effect - of physical sensation when he should have felt absolutely nothing - was like drifting in the ocean only to slam up against an unforeseen buoy.

He looked down to see a thick black coil around his waist - or where his waist should have been. He had only a moment to stare in bewilderment before he was dragged swiftly, rattlingly backwards.

The hole swallowed him. The sunlit dunes receded through the mouth of the cave. Within, there was nothing but black - but the black was moving.

He looked up, and found himself faced by a pair of fascinated golden eyes.

"How are you doing that?" he blurted out. "How can you see me? How can you hold me?"

The eyes loomed larger, closer. They were as tall as he was.

"Look at you!" said a voice from beyond them. "You're so little, even in your dreams. And pink. Not a scale on you! Tell me, is this a peculiar vision of yourself, or is this the reality of your physical form?"

"I could ask you the same thing," he said. "What are you?" It was dark, but he saw undulating, purple-black curves all around him.

"I asked first, little ghost," it said. "But I suppose I've made you my guest, so I will be polite. I am a creature of this world. You are not. Where do you come from?"

"The Clearian city," he said.

"Before that." The voice almost purred, like a cat's.

"I come from another planet."

"Another planet," it said. "How peculiar. Still, I believe it. There are peculiar things in your mind." It paused, and its eyes shifted. "What is a 'cheeseburger'?"

"It's a- listen, will you let me go if I tell you?"

There was a rumbling sound. Laughter? Or a growl?

"I'm sorry to say, little ghost, but I didn't seize you for conversation alone. There is little life on this world, and I must consume what I can, no matter how attractively peculiar."

"How can you consume me?" So far separated from his body, fear never reached him, and puzzlement dominated. "I'm only-" He paused. Only what? Only air? Only spirit?

"I could seize you, couldn't I?" It drew closer. "I admit, I'd rather have flesh, but Clearians are in short supply since they planted their noxious flowers. I can't approach the city without breaking out in hives, and they never stray far-"

"There are Clearians out in the desert," he interrupted. "Right now. I could take you to them."

"Really?" The voice was thoughtful. "What has made them so uncautious?"

"It's me," he said. "I escaped their city."

"To escape to your other planet," mused the voice. "Just like a Clearian to take it so personally." It sounded enormously amused. "This is quite a story. Fair enough, little ghost, take me to your pursuers." Its hold on him loosened. "Don't attempt to flee. It will be useless."

He floated up out of its grip. Not looking away from

those golden eyes, he backed out and zipped away from the cave. He stopped and turned to see the creature emerging.

It was enormous. Snakelike, it uncoiled leisurely, sunlight reflecting off shimmering black scales, and a single, huge golden eye regarded him as it stretched and rotated the neck of a blunt reptilian head. Two massive, muscular forearms gripped the rock. A seemingly endless expanse of tail slid continuously from the cave.

The tip of the tail eventually slipped free, and then it launched itself from the rock wall.

It flew as he did, as if it had no weight. It body undulated through the air, and its tail coiled and whipped at the end. A long thick shadow, like a river, followed below.

He led the way. The Clearians were nowhere to be seen on the track back to his body. Had they given up, or had they found him?

The cave appeared undisturbed as he flew down to it. Above him, the creature circled leisurely, drifting slowly to the entrance.

His body lay inside. Untouched. He approached it gingerly, and looked down at the face.

Drooling. Eyelids fluttering. Alive.

For a moment, he wondered what it dreamed while he was away, and then looked up just as the creature's head bridged the lip of the cave. It slid in, all the way in, gliding past him to fill every nook with its vast body. There was barely enough room for its bulk. When it was fit snug, it touched his body curiously with its blunt nose.

"Just as pink and as small," it said. "Are you a fully grown creature?"

"Almost," he said, and slipped back into his body.

Immediately he wished he hadn't. Groaning, he rolled over and spat dirt out of his mouth. His feet were raw, and his ears and the back of his neck were sunburnt to blistering. Severe, grinding hunger struck him, followed swiftly by a heavy thirst.

"You must have lived on a kind planet," remarked the

creature. "For your species to have survived."

"Yeah," he said. His voice came out raspy and faint.

"So tell me, little ghost," it said. "Where are the Clearians?"

"Close," he said. "Somewhere close."

"Ahh," it said. "So you don't know. You were only speculating that they might be nearby."

"It wasn't speculation, I know they're after me." He rolled over, and froze. The massive head was directly overhead, many times as large as his entire body. The head was tilted, one eye fixed on him, so close he could touch it. The color was brilliant. Sheer, shining gold, split through with a thin slice of black. It was an expressive eye. Speculative. Hungry.

He could see his entire reflection.

Fear flooded him. His mouth tasted sandy, bloody, and sour, and his gut roiled.

Instinctively he tried to recoil, but there was nothing but stone against his back.

"They're out there," he said.

"Perhaps," it said. "But this is not a kind planet. I must consume what I can, or I will die soon." There was faint sympathy in its voice. "You should have stayed home, little ghost."

"Wait-"

It opened its mouth, and the lining of it, all the way to the back of the throat, was barbed with teeth. They thrust from every inch, as black and shining as its scales. He screamed.

There came a soft, muffled crunching. The creature hesitated. Its eye shifted.

His mind seized wildly on the sound - footsteps?

The creature exploded over the top of him. It shot out, striking something with a painful, screaming crunch, its belly streaming overhead endlessly as it emptied itself from the cave. He watched dumbly as the tip of the tail passed over him. Something screamed repeatedly.

He rolled over onto his stomach again. Crawling pathetically, feeling as if he couldn't move any other way, he crept to the lip of the cave.

The group of Clearians was being rent apart. He saw the creature seize one, heard the howls, saw it toss the Clearian back in a single gulp and dive for another. It had a Clearian in each clawed hand and two twisted up in its tail. Blood ran sleekly in the channels between the scales around its mouth.

He watched for half a minute longer, and then he shrank back into the cave. He felt weak, and hungry.

It felt like hours, but it took the creature only minutes to eat the whole group of Clearians.

This time, when it returned, it didn't curl itself into the cave. Instead, it rested its head on the lip next to him. Its body stretched out in the sun, soaking up light, as a number of Clearian-sized bumps made their way slowly towards the tail. Its eye was nearly fully-lidded with the contentment of any well-fed animal.

"Thank you, little ghost," it said. "I think now I can expect to survive the year."

"You're welcome," he said. His voice sounded thin.

"Perhaps I can help you, now," said the creature. "I don't believe you have the strength to reach your ship. Where is it? I will take you."

"I don't know." He looked at his hands. Out of the corner of his eye, he saw blood pooling in the sand, dribbling from the corner of the creature's mouth.

"Perhaps I can find it. What does the ship look like?"

"It's big," he said. "And it's purple. And it's round."

"Ahh!" it said, sounding pleased. "I believe I've seen it."

It raised its head. There was the sound of shifting sand, and then a set of great claws were encircling him, and it lifted him off the ground. His gut plunged at the sudden ascent. He grabbed at the scaly fingers, and looked down. He gulped and had to close his eyes as they lifted off, the ground falling rapidly away. The height and the speed were so much worse from inside his body.

He didn't open his eyes for the entire trip. He clung

uselessly to the claws, feet dangling, mouth dry and heart racing. The sun was beating down on his eyelids. The wind was fierce and tore at him.

He felt progressively fainter. The air thinned. The heat, the exhaustion, the fear, and the hunger bore down upon him. He felt his mind drifting, and he blurred, somewhere half in and half out of his body. There he remained, safely unconscious, until they touched down.

"Wake up, little ghost, I have found your ship."

He jolted back to himself as they set down with a thump. The creature released him, and he collapsed immediately into the dirt. It looked down at him, paused, and then picked him up again and put him more gently onto his feet. That time he stayed up.

The ship rose up high before him, jaunty and purple. The long zigzag of a receiving rod protruded from the top like an errant cowlick. 'THE ELVIS' was printed twenty feet tall on its side, accompanied by a caricature of a man with a tall poof of black hair and a wink.

"Oh, thank you." Exhaustion aside, he ran to it, and thumped against the side with spread arms as if he could hug it. The metal was cool. Above him, the creature touched the caricature with a claw.

"Fascinating," it said.

He had been set down close to the doors, and they opened with only a faint grind of dust. The inside of the ship was immaculate. Everything was just as he had left it.

He made a beeline for the freezer.

There was a row of wadded packages on the bottom shelf, and he seized one and popped it in the reheater. Thirty seconds later, he yanked it open, ripped the wrapper off, and bit deep into a cheeseburger.

Back to the fridge, he sank down to the floor and closed his eyes. He took bite after blissful bite.

"So that's a cheeseburger."

He opened his eyes. The creature had somehow managed to get its head and shoulders through the doors, and the rest had followed. The hall was built to accommodate deliveries of massive pieces of equipment, but still, the thing barely fit. Beyond the hall, the space widened into the general bay, where he sat against the fridge, and where the creature now raised its head high above to inspect the lights. Its jaw was curved in a definite smile. It turned to look down at him.

"May I try one?" it asked. "It has a curious smell."

Mutely, he nudged the freezer door open with his foot, reached in to grab one, and scooted over to the microwave. Reaching up, he popped open the door and popped in the package, all without getting fully off the floor.

The microwave dinged.

The creature dropped to his level as he unwrapped the burger. It opened its mouth a sliver, the tips of a few visible teeth glinting under the fluorescents, and he popped the burger in. It may as well have been a jellybean.

The creature closed its mouth. There was a single jawing motion, and then he figured the burger was gone. He heard the creature made an appreciative grumbling noise.

It rose again. Twisting midair, it lifted itself up to the loft that held the control and viewing platform. It looked at the clear blue sky reflected on the viewscreen.

"Little ghost, I think you should take me with you," it said.

"What?" he said, with a choke, coughing around his burger.

"I've been of great help to you." It faced him. "I found your ship, and I rescued you from the Clearians."

"Yes, by eating them instead of me!"

"Exactly," it said, undeterred. "And little ghost, I fed well today, but this planet cannot sustain me for very longer." Its tone was solemn. "I would like to find a kinder planet."

"How do I know you won't just eat me?"

"I promise not to eat you," it said, humoring him. "I ate so well today, I feel I can go without for several months. And," it added, resting its head down next to him. There was a laugh in the back of its voice. "It looks like you have plenty of cheeseburgers."

He looked down at his last bite. He gulped it down without chewing, like the creature had the Clearian. He got to his feet, wiping dirt pointlessly on his dirty pants.

"All right," he said. "But I'm driving."

Edited by Sam Taylor

WHAT THE HELL IS THIS FOR?

By Steve Guest

"You all know why I've called you here," said the captain of the 'Sierra Longhorne Rothberg,' the first faster than light-speed mining vessel. He continued, "We need to sort the matter out immediately. So we can get back to real duties, and get this load home to a desperately needy Earth.

"That idiot foreman Somes insists that the mining crew be allowed to use the officers' toilets on 'A Deck.' He claims that there was a unanimous 'yes' vote at last night's card game, to the question that the mining crew be allowed to use the one closer to the galley, as theirs on 'D' is too far for convenience."

"Are you serious?" enquired the navigator with more than a hint of exasperation in his voice. "These bloody rock monkeys are getting us to seriously discuss saving them a seven second elevator ride for their two week trip back to earth?"

Before the captain could calm the laughter, a piece of loose rock cluster the size of a cricket ball travelling at two hundred kilometres plus per second, punched a hole through the outer, inner, sub- inner, radiation damping and inner cocoon hull, fragmenting into a scattergun blast of high velocity pieces mixed with hull shards, and punching perfectly straight vector holes through all the crew present in the meeting room. These micro-fragments continued to exit the ship via their variously deviated paths.

This was a 'Rambo Class' vessel, designed to survive ludicrous odds and disasters, and this disaster was definitely more than ludicrous and up with the worst kind. The ship could cope with the breech of its integrity by simply sealing the absolute bulkhead seals of the damaged area, whilst undergoing its auto rebuild to full integrity. It just needed that interim time to pass as the Coronium tri-nitrate reacted with the exposed Nickle-titanium-gallidium-iridium substrate, as well as giving the nano-viruses time to replicate in sufficient numbers, as every schoolboy knows.

Unfortunately, the disassembling of the executive crew had no such self-repair regime, and resulted thus in a terminal stop in all of their life processes. Besides the shredding, the instant decompression definitely made things irretrievably worse. They were gone, leaving a perfectly healthy complement of twenty-six mining staff; twenty-five miners and one supervisor slash foreman (and he was just a miner that picked the short straw at the departure terminal before the mission). This foreman was little more than the liaison between the miners and the first officer. He was now the Senior officer, the Captain in fact. He had barely passed high school.

Alarms of all kinds and lights of various hues of distress were flashing, grunting and a-oogahing while an incongruously calm female voice, sounding as if she had just climbed out of a warm bath and consumed a full meal of tryptophan laden turkey on a Christmas afternoon, cooed, "Attention all crew, please take notice of this notification of a potentially catastrophic decompression and hull penetration; the hull has been penetrated and the executive conference extension has been sealed for regeneration. All executive crew are sealed in the vacuum and will be assessed for wellbeing as soon as practically possible. Meanwhile, please don't panic, everything is probably under control as far as you know. That is all, until further information becomes available."

Somes looked at all of the other men seated for the third meal of the day, all that is, except for Bradley who had been held up for seven seconds in the elevator, when he needed to travel to 'D' so as to attend the correct facility to void his bladder. He ran into the galley seven seconds later. Somes recommenced looking at the full complement of mining staff and said in a voice belying the strength of his leadership; "Fuck! Well, I, fuck! Fuck! What do we do now?"

Hanson, sitting to his immediate left, ventured, "Wait?"

"Wait for what?" replied Somes.

Stiles said; "Well you're the senior officer, so what do we do?"

Somes, looking quite lost and perplexed said "What? What are you saying? Me, yes meem, mime in charge, I'm in charge. Okay everybody calm down! Calm down, stop panicking, ok, ok, ok, um let's see if any of the execs survived."

The calm voice of the alarm came back on with; "They didn't, they are all dead. I have just checked, and they are all definitely dead."

The alarms stopped, and the cool voice said; "Ship is secure, all damaged areas sealed and repairs under way."

Somes asked the computer what to do next, but the computer answered that she didn't know and that she was just the emergency announcement computer, only capable of assessing ship damage and state of repair, telling you the local time and the relative time on Earth, all to within a nanosecond, as well as having an interesting banter capability.

The main computer that could assist with decision making was housed in the executive area that had suffered the damage. Unfortunately, as much as the technology for self-repair was ship-wide, it was only for non-electronic metal surfaces and structures, thus the ship was without the 'Alpha level auto captain device' that could deal with almost any situation that may arise.

Somes was feeling queezy. He didn't welcome responsibility in the relatively simple role he was assigned, let alone making decisions regarding the lives of others.

Somes asked the emergency computer what direction they were heading, and if their flight homeward was still on course. The computer replied, "No idea, but the nanovirus hull work has begun as the level had surpassed thirty five trillion replications."

Somes asked Bradley and Stiles to accompany him to the bridge to see what they might be able to do. Wisely, the captain had the navigator put the ship into "Auto-Nav" while there was no one on the bridge. Fortunately enough, as a semi-executive liaison, Somes had a pass key to the bridge.

***

Somes and his companions stared blankly at the array of switches, buttons, keyboards and various input and display devices, that anyone versed in space navigation would be familiar with, but those that were familiar with the joystick of a crawler-digger had little chance of understanding. These men were expert at understanding the joystick controls of their mining devices and even more expert at not understanding this array.

Somes asked the men if any of them had experience with computers and keyboards. Stiles said that he was a Macrosoft Portholes expert and would look for a help file or online instruction manual. After some klakety-kliking, he said, "Yep, here we go. I found the online help system, with all of the instruction we need to sort this mess out."

Somes said to open the file immediately so they could get things happening. Stiles was so proud of himself and wouldn't shut up about how clever he was and what an expert he was, when in fact he had an antique machine at home that was almost five months old, and a clear two point upgrade behind on the operating system. He knew very Little in practice, other than how to point and click. But being the expert, he said that first he should make a backup of the file, so if anything went wrong, his cleverness would save them. Somes agreed and Stiles highlighted the file and pressed the option key and with a flourish of circular motion of the right hand, finger extended, brought it filmy down on the "d" key.

The computer voice asked in a slightly uncertain voice; "Are you sure you want to do this operation? If so hit enter." Feeling smug and elevating himself even higher by condescending to the device that would have the audacity to question whether or not he wanted to perform the task that he had just requested, Stiles chided the computer with; "Yes, yes I'm bloody absolutely sure I want to duplicate the file!

What do you think I am? An idiot? A simple electric thing like you with no real brain? Ha!" He slammed the "Enter" key, initiating the series of electronic impulses that would arrange the bits as he was requesting. Obediently it was carried out in a microsecond, and the computer responded; "File deleted."

There was a deafening silence, and a hot flush rolled over Stiles as he looked in dismay at the monitor. "No!" he screamed. "No, you stupid bitch! Not delete! Duplicate! No, no wait, Duplicate is Control-Option-D. What did I hit? ...I hit Option-D." His head started to spin as the gravity of his faux pas started to reveal itself like a tsunami heading for him on the beach of Misery.

In an elegant display of the art of using ego defence mechanisms and the protection of his subconscious psyche, Stiles cleared his mind, smiled, cleared his throat, pushed himself away from the console and gestured gracefully, with a slight bow to Somes saying that he, Somes, should just give it a bat, step up to the crease with confidence and push some buttons to familiarise himself with the controls. The apparent lack of wisdom of this approach was apparently lost on Somes and his friends. Still not quite comprehending what had just transpired, Somes sat himself into the navigator's seat. At this point he turned to Stiles and enquired as to where the help file was, the one that was going to save them. Stiles , "Ahh, well, yes, you see, it's errr... it's gone."

"Gone?" echoed the other two.

"Yep, gone, gone, gone, gone forever, never to return, it doesn't exist anymore, it's gone, as I have completely deleted it. Silly me," Stiles replied with a slight smile, his mind refusing to allow him to suffer the indignity of understanding the magnitude of his error.

Somes said, "Wo... bu... what... w... um, do, w..." but tailed off into a mist of non-comprehension.

In a semi-dazed and more bewildered state, Somes turned back to the panel and looked for inspiration. He pressed the large red button. He did this because it was the biggest button, and it had the word "Emergency" engraved and filled with yellow right across the dome of its shiny plastic knob.

Immediately the engines shut down. The cool voiced computer broke the anticipatory silence with a smooth, "Engines off, navigation disengaged. Please enter sequence Gamma Omega to reinitiate course and restart engines." There was a few more seconds' silence and a further tightening of the three men's sphincters, and the voice announced the worrying question, "There is no apparent system emergency, why did you disengage? This action is not advised unless imminent structural or engine malfunction is confirmed? Please restart engines."

The three men were sweating and the rise in pitch of their voices showed there was little control amongst them. They looked frantically for a button that might give rise to a start-up sequence, but the only other button of note was a purple recessed button that was labelled 'SLR – DESTRUCT.' It had a carefully placed yellow 'Post-it' note written in the authoritative, if not untidy hand of the captain, placed immediately under it, reading 'Do not press this button under ANY circumstances!!!' It was also signed by the captain.

Bradley cautioned Somes to avoid pressing the purple button at all costs, particularly as it was a written standing order from the ex-captain, who knew what he was doing. Secondly, the captain underlined it and put the 'Any' in capitals, finishing with not one exclamation mark, but three. That emphasised in a rhetorical manner the importance of the statement preceding these peculiarly powerful marks, that end a statement that is meant to be understood as not just mere chit-chat, but an exclamation. And as if in a formal threat to enact some form of punishment if disobeyed, the captain signed it not only with his name, which would have been enough to instil compliance in the bravest and most non-compliant crew member, but also added the weight of formal threat by putting his rank of senior officer, being that of the Captain.

They were in enough trouble without initiating a destruct

sequence of the Sierra Longhorne Rothberg, especially while they were in it. It stood to their feeble reason that it couldn't be good or the least bit helpful in their particular situation. Stiles pointed out that he couldn't quite fathom any situation where you would need a self-destruct button on any ship. Bradley countered with the fact that all of the best movies about spaceships had a self destruct function for various good reasons.

Somes called the men to concentrate on the task at hand, while he went off to 'D' deck. But then he realised that there was no one to stop him going to the much closer 'A', so he went there, not bothering to inform the other two. After all they were busy trying to concentrate on not being in this terrible situation, and he didn't want to distract them... So he didn't, he just went. He thought he could tell them at a later time when things were hopefully better, and if not, at least when the anxiety of the moment had passed. This was how Somes occupied his thinking life, a practical, simple man, if a bit off point at times.

Upon his return from his short journey to where the others didn't know because he had led them to believe he was going elsewhere but changed his mind without informing them, because they were busy, Somes asked the men to take all of the written material and go through it with a fine tooth comb to see if there were some instructions about starting the engines and pointing the ship home. The men did this with an earnest undertaking, and although there was many a technical detail, they were certain after weeks of reading and rereading that there was absolutely nothing there about sailing this ship. There were instructions on the micro-mist decontamination showers, sonic toothbrush warranties, and a manual describing the various emotional states that space flight can cause. There were manuals on the maintenance and repair of food integrators and a book on the dangers of exposure to unscreened tanti-radiation from un-shielded hair removal devices. But nothing on the way to get home.

The life support systems were capable of producing

enough fresh water. As the ship was a closed system, the water that was with them from day one would always be available, as they eventually excreted the liquid one way or another, and the food was obviously formed through the atomic reconstruction method via the 'From Poo 2 U © 2237' food integrators. The oxygen, nitrogen and other necessary gases were rebound and recirculated as they always were, so survival wasn't a problem, and because sickness in all its forms had been eradicated by the Monsanta company over a hundred years ago, life was assured.

***

There were only semi educated, roughneck men aboard, and after three years adrift in deep space, they were really, really shitting each other off, more than could be reasonably tolerated by any man, let alone short tempered, testosterone laiden, ill-rationed of wit and insight, vertical thinking miners, not that all miners are of lesser intelligence, but, well, actually, pretty much all miners are quite thick, it's a bit of a job prerequisite really. I mean, who in their right mind would want to slug their day out digging up rocks and moving them about? It's not rocket science. Well in fact it is, because it's done in deep space, on lonely asteroids, but you know what I'm getting at. It's a job that a droid with ninety-seven lines of well written code could pull off, and if it wasn't for the unions, that's exactly what all miners would be; twelve thousand dollars' worth of nano-circuitry, eight bucks worth of flexi drive polymer musculature, a titanium endo-exoskeleton and a nice paint job with the company logo on the chest.

This lack of advanced social and organisational abilities led to many hostile confrontations, breaches of etiquette of all codes, nine deaths and a large salad bowl with the outline of a poor sod's face slightly deforming it being the least damaged moveable appliance in the ship. That made a peaceful cooperative attempt to work a way back to Earth, a literal impossibility.

Somes barely kept any semblance of order and if it wasn't

for his occasional threat to press the purple Sierra Longhorne Rothberg Destruct button, he would have no authority whatsoever. The 'Brig' was set up from the sick bay and expanded room by room the longer the disgruntled lot spent drifting in space. And as men confined with few pleasures have done for centuries, they distilled and consumed alcohol in adequate quantities to ensure rational behaviour was an exception to the norm.

Many philosophies developed amongst the crew, although it would be a hard struck task to argue the term 'philosophers' was a fitting title to the practitioners of these found-upon ways of being, doing and thinking. For example, Richards, a leathered fifty-two year old Shropshireman from England, came to the conclusion that it was because of a crime against nature that he committed as a pubescent lad on his father's farm with a poddy calf, that this celestial punishment, by celestial gods, that visited him in his dreams was being metred out in unmerciful measure.

It was in one of the morphean visitations that he was given the key to eternal salvation, and it was this wisdom that was imparted; be naked and apologise for everything to everyone all of the time. He was one of the most unpopular men aboard by year two and was very fortunate to be alive according to Brunton. Brunton was another Englishman that grew to believe that there is no good nor evil, just that 'what happened' was reality and you dealt with it as it came. He was a sort of existentialist, but he did like people praising his good judgement. He was also hated.

Then there was Eric Wilde a paranoid Dubliner, convinced that it was a plot by the mining company that put them in this dilemma, and that everyone there but he, were innocent bystanders, except for a few (well, nine) 'company spies,' the lowest forms of life. One day after a particularly heavy bout of wine tasting, he liberated these nine from the constant need to breathe, in a merciless 'Cleansing of the traitor class.'

The rest of the men were just content with being drunk,

singing and playing cards for ludicrous stakes with debts for some in the hundreds of trillions of dollars. Laws were formed, but no one took much notice, and the brig just became the living quarters for the most socially reprehensible practitioners of violence and abuse and they were under their own recognisance.

***

Somes, Stiles and Bradley sat in the bridge watching an episode of 'I Love Lucy' from the ship's universal database of entertainment. It contained every television show, every movie and documentary, every piece of music, every recording ever made by man. Somes loved redheads.

Bradley was distracted. He was thinking about how he could win back the bazillion dollars he owed the Dubliner for his latest loss at poker, when he noticed a glinting object moving across the field of view of the rewindow that formed the front of the bridge. He watched with rising curiosity as it came to a halt and seemed to grow in size and intensity of glint. 'Could it be moving towards us,' he wondered quietly. He pushed the zoom slider on the rewindow control and in crisp focus was a beautifully elegant spacecraft. A deep purple sheen skinned a sleek cube with various appendages of a mechanical nature prickling from the surface. The reading on the rewindow told him that the object was only twenty eight million kilometres away and approaching at forty two million kilometers per hour. He did some quick maths and yelled; "They'll be here in about an hour and a half!"

Somes, lost in Lucy, spilled his Chickenesque Soup in his lap and knocked the big red button on the console. Stiles just looked confused. The cool voice of the computer said, "You have already pressed that button, pressing it again will not help, thank you."

Somes wiped himself and the seat with an old bit of shirt he had hanging out of his pocket, as Bradley, excitedly bobbing up and down like a child that needed a wee really badly, pointed to the rewindow. All three stared at the purple cube, and spontaneously grabbed each other in a group hug, bouncing up and down in a threesome of urinary urgency.

Somes broke free as the universal frequency comms sounded. Garbled noise came through, but it was recognisable as a language, it had repetition and a rise in tone when the gobbledygook was repeated. The talk button was labeled 'Send' so Somes slammed it down and yelled, "Help! Help us, we're lost in space, we are lost... in, um, space. Help! Welcome, come in!"

Somes wasn't quite on best form for communicating with a foreign species. He could barely hold a coherent conversation with his own. The comms went quiet as the craft rapidly approached. Somes made a few more attempts to communicate with phrases like; "we happy you find us" and "our home far away, we no can get home, you help us get home."

Stiles remarked that his attempt at talking to them in broken English was probably futile, unless the particular species had worked in a Chinese restaurant taking orders from drunken Americans.

So they sat and waited. Somes put out a general call over the ship's intercom, informing of the approaching craft. Presently all seventeen men assembled in the bridge to await their hoped-for rescue. There was a lot of conjecture and 'what ifs.' There were tears and whoops of joy. Some were wary of the unknown factor in the box hurtling towards them, but to a man there was intense interest.

***

The craft was huge as it sat in front of the mining vessel. Lights throbbed and things moved behind frosted semitransparent ovals that looked like massive eyes on the ship.

Again the comms sounded with the strange language. This time it was clearly more insistent, almost threatening. A few of the men left the bridge for who knows where, while others just gawped in awe.

Somes once more responded with "What? I can't understand you. Do you speak English, Australian or

American?"

The ship started to move back ever so slowly. When it was about a kilometre away, two huge armatures unfolded from the top corners of the massive cube. Identical, both arms extended at a forty-five degree angle to the sides of the cube, to a length of about two hundred metres. Articulating about half way down, the top half of each arm narrowed to a point and bloomed three parabolic dishes of thirty metres diameter each, evenly spaced along the upper part of the arm. The upper arms folded forward pointing directly at the ship, the line of each meeting right at the bridge of the mining vessel. Somes muttered, "We're gonna die."

A blinding light shot out of the parabolic dishes, brilliant orange in the centre with an ionising blue to the outer edge of the ray.

Everyone in the bridge except for Somes panicked and ducked for cover, hiding behind seats and consoles, dustbins and cabinets, and each other. But just as Somes felt a bit of wee come out, the flashes stopped and two alien life forms appeared on the bridge in front of him and the cowering mob.

The aliens gestured with open, what were more than likely, palms that supported three finger like appendages that were more than likely, fingers. They then knelt and bowed their, what were probably, heads. They were communicating that they were not hostile. They then stood and walked to Somes, as he was the only one not cowering behind cover of some type.

They both touched him, and in a similar gesture of non threatening behaviour, Somes gave them the 'Thumbs up.' The aliens looked at this gross movement of what they thought were probably fingers, looked at each other, made some funny language noises and shrugged what was probably their shoulders and started to point at the consoles. Somes correctly interpreted this as a question, and gesticulated a thumbs down. There was no response from the visitors, so he grabbed a plastic ruler from the console, pointed to the console and then to the whole ship, pointed to the ruler and snapped the ruler in half and dropped it, then jumped on the pieces, imploring the aliens to understand that the ship was as broken as the ruler.

One of the aliens, the good looking one, pointed at the console, the ship and the ruler and picked up the ruler, and pointed the broken ruler at the console and ship, throwing the ruler into the air and letting it fall to the floor. It was becoming clear that the aliens understood the concept, and the uglier one tapped Somes on the chest and pointed to both itself and its companion, then to its ship, then to all present, again to its ship, then made a swift gesture to space.

Somes told everyone that these good creatures were going to help them, it was clear that they understood the predicament.

The alien pointed at each man there and made a noise with each point. Then repeated the last noise he made, then pointed to himself and his partner making the same noises he started with.

One of the miners said, "He just counted us, then he counted him and his mate."

Somes then counted his men one by one out loud, then the two aliens, numbering to total, just as the alien had done. He noticed that there was one man missing; the Dubliner, Wilde was missing. Somes thought to himself that he was probably hiding because he was after all quite mad and paranoid. He then pointed to the aliens' craft and recounted the aliens "one, two," then pointed at the craft outside and continued with a bouncing finger "three, four, five?"

The cute alien grabbed his arm to stop him counting, and mimicked his count by holding Somes' finger and made an attempt to count as Somes had "arn, oow, arn, oow, arn, oow," backwards and forwards between he and his companion. Somes was catching on. Maybe it was the adrenaline surge heightening his feeble mind, but he understood that there were no other aliens on board.

The aliens started bobbing up and down a little like they

were happy with these communications.

Somes announced that this called for a celebration, that they would show their guests the food that they had along with the variety of drinks and share them if the visitors found anything edible.

Everyone was milling around happily chatting in the galley. The two 'saviours' were sitting on a table, slightly elevated from the seated in a gesture of respect. They fortunately found the foods palatable and the drinks imbibable, and everyone was happy.

The cute alien stood and made a speech that was of absolutely no meaning to any of the ship's complement, but taken in the spirit it was being delivered in, with "hear, hears" and "Amens" nodding of heads and all the appropriate agreeable showings, when a loud "crack-crack" rang out from the rear door of the galley. Everyone turned to see the mad Dubliner wielding a plasma gun, screaming "Got the murderous conspiratorial bastards!"

Two perfect shots had opened the big things at the top of the aliens' bodies, that all had correctly assumed was their heads, and an orangey limey mess was splattered all over the galley wall and the men close by.

Wilde was set upon, and put into a food integrator.
***

Months passed and the morale of the men declined to an all-time low. There were two suicides and many alcoholic comas. Richards became so despondent, he proclaimed to all that there were no gods and put his pants back on.

Somes and Stiles sat in the bridge, as was their wont, watching 'Wildest Police Videos' when Somes got up and said that he couldn't take it any more. He said "I'm pushing the button." He walked towards the console. Stiles hadn't had enough, he still wanted to live regardless of the situation. He tackled Somes just as he was reaching for the SLR DESTRUCT button. He knocked Somes clear, but Somes wasn't giving up that easily and knocked Stiles hard, back against a wall. Somes made it to the console. There was nothing Stiles could do, he was too shaken to move rapidly. He begged Somes to reconsider, and give it just a few more days.

Somes laughed out loud and focused on the purple button. He noticed that the captain's post-it note had been dislodged in the fracas between he and Stiles. There was writing on a boilerplate under the button. It had been obscured for all of these years. Somes read it and asked Stiles to come and read it just so he could be sure he understood it.

It read; 'In case of critical failures of ship's navigation or engine systems, press and hold this SLRDESTRUCT button to engage the Ships Life Raft Deploy Engine Startup & Return Using Computed Trajectory system. Life Raft mode will be enabled. The vessel will return to base using auxiliary engines and fuel. All previous navigation will be overridden. Estimated travel time will be under two weeks from anywhere in the galaxy. CAUTION: Use only in the case of valid emergency.'

Both men read it, reread it, then read it again. Somes turned to Stiles and said, "Well, we had better press it then..."

Edited by Sam Taylor

TIME WILL TELL

By Tim McLean

I hope someone is reading this, if not then I'm wasting my time. It's most likely been a few weeks – maybe even months – since I did my little disappearing act. To be fair, I haven't actually done it yet, but I will have by the time you start reading. Using past tense to talk about things you're going to do in the future is a little weird. Maybe I shouldn't have locked myself away in the house for so long. Not only has it caused me to ramble on and on in my writing, but people have gotten used to not seeing me, which probably means it'll take a while before I'm missed. For all I know you could be reading this years after I wrote it. If Hector is still hanging around the house then please feel free to feed him. I had planned to take him to the shelter but he's out somewhere and I'm running out of time. The cat flap is unlocked and I've never known a better hunter, so I'm pretty sure he'll be just fine without me.

If you're familiar with my work then you probably know what I've done. If you aren't then please grab the notebook I've left on my desk (right beside the thing you're reading right now) and take it to Dr Evans down at the university. Make sure you shove it up his backside and tell him that he was wrong and I was right. Maybe I should've sent it to him in the post . . . no time for that now.

It's a little ironic really. Here I am running out of time, just before activating my time machine. It's pretty funny when you really think about it. After all, I could probably use it to go back in time and post the letter. Better yet, I could just go back and tell my historical self all the tricks to get the stupid thing working a little earlier. I won't bore you with the details of all the technical problems now, though. Everything is in the notebook, just look there.

You're probably wondering how I got to this point. Even

if you're not I'm going to write the story down anyway. Maybe by the time I finish, Hector will be back and he can see me off.

It started just a year ago with me and Evans discussing different time travel theories. He's willing to admit that it is at least potentially possible, so he deserves a little credit for that. It's just a shame that he thinks I'm a lunatic. He didn't believe a single word I said to him. I explained that my machine was almost ready to be tested, but when I showed it to him all he saw was three computers hooked up to a satellite dish. Of course that's what he saw, how could he see anything else? I mean, the machine is three computers hooked up to a satellite dish. You have to look past that and see what I've done with it. You're reading this in my laboratory now, so see for yourself. Actually, don't turn it on. Either wait until you've finished reading or until you've spoken to Evans. Trust me, it's safer that way.

So, anyway, Evans called me a maniac and we had a bit of an argument, which pretty much killed our friendship. I told him if he came back in a couple of weeks then he'd see the machine in action, but he wasn't having any of that. I distinctly remember him mocking me, saying, "Does it work on the Terminator or the Back to the Future model?"

What a prick.

If a friend of yours invited you to their house in a couple of weeks to see an Actual-Working-Fucking-Time-Machine, would you go? I know I would. Not Evans. Oh no, not high and mighty Doctor Evans. He writes for Theoretical Physics Monthly now. Well, I made that title up, but it's got some pretentious name like that. Y'know, something sciencey. I've forgotten what it's really called and I honestly couldn't care less. Evans is in the past and I'll soon be in the future.

Even though he completely dismissed my claims, Evans gave me the idea of how to test the machine. It's impossible to see if travelling to the future is possible. What you can do (what I indeed did do) is send things to the past and see if they turn up in the present. It sounds a little simpler than it actually is.

I used the same method every single time I tried it. I took a coin with this year's date on it and sent it back to around a thousand years ago, not always that far but I really like the idea of some Dark Age savage finding Queen Elizabeth II's face on a coin. Not that it mattered, I never had any luck. Obviously it's possible that someone did find my coins and kept them, or at least moved them away from the area of where my house would one day be. If I had worked it all out right, the coins should have been buried in my back garden somewhere, preserved in the ground. I even bought a metal detector to help me find them. Not a crappy cheap one mind you, it cost me a small fortune! After many unsuccessful searches, I started to think that maybe I was just somehow dematerialising the coins with the machine. Then I had the genius idea of just sending the coins back by a few minutes. Obviously that didn't work. It just looked like the coins remained in the same place. The only way I could have known if it worked would be if I'd been in the past and saw them materialise in front of me. But I don't remember that ever happening.

Sending things back always gave me a strange feeling. What if the coin just happened to appear inside some poor, unsuspecting person? I never wanted to harm anyone so I stopped doing that. I'm not entirely sure why I thought sending things to the future wouldn't work. I was thinking on too grand a scale. All I really had to do was calibrate the machine to send things a few minutes forward and wait for them to appear.

That's what I did, and it worked!

I remember sitting there the first time, watching as the coin disappeared. I sat waiting for a long time. The coin should have reappeared in the exact same spot that it vanished from, but it didn't. Clearly that's where I was going wrong. I'd assumed that it wouldn't move in any other dimension except the fourth: time itself. The thing was, the location changed too. Strangely enough, the coin reappeared on my bathroom windowsill. Weird. My calculations never allowed for regular teleportation as well as time travel. Not that it really matters.

I'd taken the time to gather a whole bunch of coins from this year; fifty pence ones are my favourite. Unfortunately that made things quite expensive when I sent them to the past, especially since I have no income at the moment. I should've just used pennies. Anyway, I repeated the experiment a few more times and every time I did the coins reappeared in different places: on my bedside cabinet, on the mantelpiece, beside the front door, pretty much everywhere in the house that I can think of. It seemed completely random, almost as though I had just accidentally dropped them there. For a time I wondered if maybe that was what had happened, but I'm not that stupid. I know I don't just randomly drop coins around the house. But I did find some that I don't remember sending. Maybe I'll send some from the future, but I have no way of knowing that until I go.

Truth be told, I'm a little apprehensive about using the machine on myself. What if I materialise inside a brick wall or deep under the sea? That would ruin my day completely. Maybe I should just jump forward a minute or so the first time, just to test it. Actually, maybe I should send Hector instead! I could never forgive myself if I harmed him though, so it really has to be me.

I still don't understand why sending the coins back a few minutes didn't cause them to appear in a random place in the house. It doesn't make any sense. Why does sending things forward cause them to move?

Screw it; I'm not going to think about that. That's just the way it is and I need to get a move on. You probably don't even realise why I'm in such a rush, and how could you know?

I have a brain tumour. Apparently it's inoperable. Evans reckons it's made me delusional, but he's wrong. I'm focused and I know exactly what I have to do. Doctors these days don't have a clue. For a start they gave me six months to live and I've been around for over a year since then. What do they know? Once I get to the future they'll be able to help me. Humanity takes giant technological leaps in every century, so I'm guessing a couple of hundred years should do the trick. And if by some chance they haven't worked out how to cure me by then, I'll just build a new time machine and travel further into the future. With any luck the National Health Service will still exist then, otherwise the operation might turn out to be hellishly expensive. At least I should have accumulated plenty of interest from my bank account by then. What have I got to lose? I can stay here and let the cancer destroy me or I can stand in front of the satellite dish and press the 'enter' button. For all I know I might only have a few moments to live. I'm basically on borrowed time. That's exactly how they put it. But borrowed from whom?

Well . . . from me, of course. I have the power to lend myself as much time as I need.

A thought just occurred to me. Not only can I travel back in time and take my rightful place at the top of the scientific ladder as the inventor of time travel when all this is done, but I could also take the cure for cancer back with me. Think about all the good I could do with my device. I will be the saviour of the human race! I'll do what Jesus couldn't. Sure, he might save your eternal soul (if such a thing even exists and if Jesus was even a real person), but I will prolong earthly existence for millions of people. Then I can really shove it into Evans's smug face.

There is of course still the slight chance that I really did accidentally drop those coins in random places around the house, and that the machine just vaporised the ones I was trying to send . . . but that's a risk I'm willing to take. With any luck vaporisation isn't all that painful. At the very least it can't be any worse than the prolonged agony of waiting for the tumour to do me in. Time will tell.

Time: If only I had more of it.

Anyway, I'm scribbling away and stalling for time now. The moment has finally come . . . it's now or never. Hector's still out, but that's okay, I'll just go without saying goodbye. I'm going to put plenty of cat food out for him, enough to last a few days. It's winter at the moment, so there isn't much of a risk of flies laying eggs on it like in the summer.

If you find this and you think it's all a load of bollocks then please feel free to do whatever you want with the equipment. Perhaps you can even use my notes to compile a science fiction story. You never know, it might make you some money!

If you live for a couple of hundred years then I might see you in the future. If I come back you can thank me for curing cancer.

I really hope the machine won't turn my body into some kind of aerosol. Time will tell.

14.12.2012

...

This is the last known work of my eminent colleague and friend, discovered in September of 2013 after concerned neighbours contacted police. George had not been seen for many months after refusing to accept treatment for his condition. Had I known how desperate things were I would have returned from Australia to help him myself. Had it not been for the smell caused by the body of George's beloved cat, Hector, I don't think anyone would ever have discovered that he'd had gone missing. Hector's remains were found amongst a bunch of broken computer monitors and the satellite dish mentioned in the article.

Although he is now presumed deceased, if anybody has information about George's whereabouts please contact your local police station. I included his entire story here so that people would have an understanding of George's state of mind. Some of his language is a little colourful, so it's possible that the newspaper will edit that. If they don't then I'm truly sorry, it is not meant to be offensive.

You were an inspiration to all who knew you, not just academically but also because of your brilliant sense of humour. You will be missed, George, and never forgotten.

A service will be held at the Washington Methodist Church on 20/10/2013.

*Obituary entry in honour of Professor George Evans.

Edited by Sam Taylor

EASY AS PI

By John Gribbin

This story is self-contained, but set in the same universe as Artifact, published in the first volume of Tales From the Perseus Arm. Put the two together, and what you get should be greater than the sum of the parts. And, yes, there is an "author's message" here; see my book In Search of the Multiverse.

The student knocked on the open door and hesitated, waiting for permission to cross the threshold.

"It's open," came the exasperated response.

He shuffled inside, holding out the Turing.

"Uh, I thought you ought to see this. It's, well, weird..."

The grey-haired man pushed his chair back from the desk and reached for the Turing. He peered at it over the top of his old-fashioned glasses, muttering inaudibly. The University, for reasons he had never been able to fathom, required all arts students to carry out a science project, which meant someone in the science faculty had to supervise them. A complete waste of time for both parties. As ridiculous as the requirement for science students to do a critical analysis of a novel. So Timmins had come up with a painless (for him) solution. The pi project. Give him a student with time to waste, and he would set the victim the task of calculating the next hundred thousand or so digits of pi. You couldn't deny it was scientific, and at a pinch you could even say it was original, since each student carried on where the previous one had left off. And since pi was irrational, every student got a different set of digits to play with, even though they were now well into the trillions – he neither knew nor cared how far into the trillions.

Every student got a different set of digits, except this idiot.

The string of numbers filled the display, but the beginning

was all too familiar

3141592653589793...

He leaned back in his chair, pushing his glasses up in order to rub his eyes.

"You were supposed, Omero, to start where Phillips left off. Not at the beginning."

"But I did. This string starts about 87,000 places into the run. And it carries on like that. What does it mean?"

"It means you pressed the wrong button. Go away and check."

"I did." This one was stubborn. "It repeats from the beginning, at least ten thousand digits."

"Then check it again. Check a hundred thousand digits, And don't come back until you've found the mistake."

Reluctantly, the student turned to go, automatically reaching for the door handle.

"And don't shut the door!"

Timmins turned back to the screen in front of him, pushing the glasses back up his nose to their proper position. He had his own computer code to worry about. Simulating star formation, if only he could make it work. There was a problem with truncation in the core collapse code. It had a tendency towards chaos – if you made a tiny change in the value of the parameters, it had a big effect on the outcome. That's the trouble with simulations, he thought – nature "knows" the values to an infinite number of places, we have to truncate the parameters.

Infinity. Something was nagging at the back of his mind. The Book of Infinity – who was it wrote that? Graves?

He opened a new window and did a search – Graves, infinity, simulation, universe.

There it was. The paragraph sat there innocently, its message unambiguous.

How could we tell if the Universe we live in is a computer simulation, like the world of the Matrix movies? The difference between a simulation and what we call reality is that simulations are approximate. They can be made as good as you like, if you have enough memory, but they can never be made perfect. An irrational number like pi can only be perfectly expressed as an infinite string of digits, which would fill up the memory of any computer on its own, and leave no room for anything else. Even the best computer does not have infinite capacity, so the programmers of a universal simulation would have to make approximations. For example, they might truncate the values of the constants used in fundamental calculations – things like e, or pi. Or the simulation might become regular instead of irrational after a high number of digits. If anyone ever finds such a regularity in one of these constants, it will be the smoking gun that tells us that nothing is real.

The smoking gun. Of course, Graves was a notorious joker. He hadn't meant to be taken seriously. Had he?

Reluctantly, Timmins accessed Omero's project, watching the numbers ticking up as they were computed. How many should he let accumulate before checking the string against the first – what, million? – digits of pi? And suppose somebody else was on to it. He suddenly felt a sense of urgency. Even a simulated Nobel Prize would be worth having, if you were a simulation yourself.

Edited by Sam Taylor

ASYLUM

By CM Martin

Someone was screaming. A book flew through the air and landed with a dull "splat" against a barred window. A naked man ran down the hall, singing "Jingle Bells" at the top of his lungs while his jingle *balls* bounced merrily in time with his strides. In a far corner of the activities room, an elderly woman was trying to eat her Raggedy Ann doll, but the head wouldn't fit in her mouth, so she settled for gnawing on the colorful yarn hair.

Dr. David Rosenberg slipped through the open door and then shut it behind him, coding the locking sequence in the pad on the wall. It was just another beautiful July morning in the Jackson County Hospital psych ward. The home, like most county hospitals, of a mixed bag of addicts, dementia patients on fixed incomes, depressives who spent their days wishing for something sharper than plastic eating utensils, and the occasional paranoid schizophrenic. The good doctor made his way through the locked ward towards his office, greeting patients and nurses along the way. He was a short, stout fellow, looking like a "cross between a hobbit and one of those Russian nesting dolls," as his partner Michael had once observed. With twinkling dark brown eyes and a kindly smile, Dr. Rosenberg looked far too happy for someone who spent his days dealing with the deranged. But then, perhaps that was why he was so very successful—he was almost never cross or out of patience, and he was invariably kind to the residents, even the most difficult ones.

"Good morning, Joan," he said as passed the bone-thin, middle-aged woman sitting on the floor, shredding the previous day's newspaper as she did each morning. Her name wasn't actually Joan; it was Joanne. She labored under the delusion that she was Joan of Arc, and each and every morning, she faithfully shredded newspapers into a pile, just in case the English arrived that day to burn her at the stake.

"I'll want plenty of fuel, you see," she'd explained to Dr. Rosenberg once, her watery blue eyes earnest in their gaze. "It hurts less if there's plenty of fuel, or so I've been told by the other martyrs who suffered as I will suffer."

Someday, David hoped, they'd be able to go deep enough into the layers of Joanne's troubled mind to convince her that she wasn't a 13th century French peasant girl in danger of being burned alive for heresy. However, until the day they found the right combination of psychotropic drugs, Joanne needed to stay in this locked ward while her anorexia and auditory hallucinations were treated. She also needed to be kept away from matches, cigarette lighters, and the kitchen stove, since she'd already set herself on fire at home twice, with fortunately minimal scarring as a result. For obvious reasons, her husband didn't want her back home until she could be trusted not to try to meet her imagined fate.

"Morning, Dr. Feelgood," another resident yelled from across the room.

"Morning, Anthony," Dr. Rosenberg replied. "How are you feeling today?"

"I'll feel one Hell of a lot better when I get my LSD dose." Anthony had lived through the '60s. Unfortunately, he'd never left. A hopeless addict with significant cognitive issues, a tendency towards fits of paranoid rage and frequent flashbacks, he too was a long-term resident of this particular ward.

"I'll speak to the nurse right away," Rosenberg promised Anthony. Several weeks ago, the good doctor had prescribed a daily ration of one dampened sugar cube for Anthony, and his fits of rage and attempts at self-harm had decreased dramatically as a result, as his seriously fried synapses told him he was getting his ride on the magic carpet. On the other hand, he was using a great deal of finger paint and paper as he spent every day "tripping", but Dr. Rosenberg considered that an acceptable trade-off.

David stopped a passing nurse. "Robin, would you make

sure Anthony gets his daily dose?" The nurse, a big-boned brunette with an air of complete world-weariness, nodded with a slight smile.

"Sure thing, doctor," she replied. "Maybe it will make him shut the fuck up and put on some clothes." Anthony was the patient who had been serenading staff and fellow patients with his sky-clad version of "Jingle Bells" as he ran through the activities room and down the hall towards the nurse's desk.

"We can only hope," David replied. He glanced around the common room. "Any new guests?"

"Just one," Robin said. "Female, approximately 35 years of age. No I.D., no apparent injuries or illness, presenting with significant paranoid delusions. She's in the intake room on suicide watch." All new patients were put into a small private room when they were first admitted, where they were kept under close observation until the staff was reasonably sure the new arrival did not pose a threat to self or others. From a medical standpoint, the staff also had to make sure that the new patient wasn't carrying TB, hepatitis, bird flu, or some other nasty bug that would infect a ward full of people with largely dysfunctional immune systems.

"No. I.D.? Who brought her in, the cops?"

Robin shook her head. "No," she replied. "That's the weird part. She wandered into the ER last night—and asked for sanctuary."

After his morning paperwork, cup of bad coffee, and group therapy session for the ward's meth addicts (always the largest group being treated at any given time), David decided he ought to see the newcomer. He buzzed the nurse's station, and Robin answered.

"What's the status of our new Jane Doe?

"I checked on her about 20 minutes ago; she's awake and just sitting on the bed looking out the window," the nurse replied. "Seems fine, except for the whole 'somebody's planning to kill me' spiel. She's sticking to that."

"Would you have someone bring her to my office?" the psychiatrist requested. "I may as well do an intake evaluation."

"Sure thing, boss," Robin replied cheerfully. "I'll walk her in myself."

"Thank you." David hung up and pulled out a lined pad of paper and a pen. He'd no sooner taken a sip of his coffee than there was a sharp rap on the door, which opened to reveal Nurse Robin and a tall, silent figure dressed in standard hospital scrubs. David got to his feet and took a couple of steps forward.

"Thank you, Ms. Van Camp." He nodded to the nurse and turned his attention to his new patient. "Won't you come in?" he asked quietly, giving her a small smile and putting as much warmth as he could into his gaze. The woman nodded and moved across the room towards the chair he'd indicated, while David watched closely. She moved slowly, her steps hesitant, as if she were tranquilized—or as if she were unacquainted with her feet. Brain lesions? The doctor thought, his mind ticking through possible diagnoses. Drug addiction, MS, advanced syphilis? Cut it out, David. He scolded himself. You're guessing, not diagnosing the problem. Observe for now. Time enough for speculation later.

The woman made it to the chair and sat down as David moved around the desk and took his seat as well. For a few moments, they simply looked at one another. David's latest patient was taller than he; he estimated she was maybe 5'11', although her shoulders were slumped, making her exact height more difficult to judge. She was quite big-boned, not fat but certainly not dainty. Her hair, chopped off right at chin length, was perhaps her best feature, slightly wavy and an extraordinary mix of red, gold, and copper. Her nose was too big for beauty and her mouth too small, but she had lovely eyes that were a dark gray instead of the expected blue of most redheads. For a long moment, she and David simply looked at one another.

"My name is Dr. David Rosenberg," he said at last. "Would you like to tell me your name?"

Unsurprisingly, she shook her head.

"Are you sure?" he persisted gently. "I'd like to notify your family, let them know you're safe."

"I have no family," she replied simply. "And you would not be able to pronounce my name."

Interesting delusion, he thought. He'd had plenty of patients who wouldn't respond to their names but never one who did so on the grounds that he wouldn't be able to pronounce it.

"Well, it would be helpful if I could call you something," David said. His new patient simply shrugged.

"As you wish."

David thought for a moment. He'd never liked the custom of referring to anonymous patients as John or Jane Doe, and he wasn't going to do it with this woman. "I'll call you...Beth," he said at last. Many years ago, David Rosenberg had had a sister named Beth. The doctors she'd been assigned to had not been able to stop her in time - it was one reason why he, David, was so determined to succeed with every patient.

His new patient nodded. "As you wish," she said once more.

For the next few days, David went about his rounds with his usual patients, while Beth Doe as she was now listed on her chart underwent her first staffing, an initial meeting with the hospital's psych team, social worker, and general physician. Rosenberg checked the daily logs, of course, and read the various nurses' and aides' notations on their mystery patient. All were in agreement: she kept to herself and ate very little, but she exhibited no violent tendencies and on the few occasions that she did interact with either staff or her fellow patients, she was unfailingly soft-spoken and courteous. She made no suicidal threats, but she continued to insist that she couldn't leave the hospital because "they" would kill her. It seemed to be her only manifestation of a psychological problem, but it was consistent—and it was troubling. Once Beth had officially been evaluated, Dr. Rosenberg decided it was time to at least confront that delusion.

In response to the soft knock on his office door, David looked up from his endless paperwork and called out, "Come in." The door opened to reveal Beth, dressed as always in hospital scrubs, since she'd arrived with no luggage, and no one had come in the days since then looking for her or bringing personal belongings.

"Beth." The psychiatrist rose to his feet and gestured towards his guest chair. "Please, come and sit down." Once again he watched as she crossed the room, the awkward hesitancy still apparent in her movements. It wasn't just his imagination; virtually every nurse and tech had commented on it. "Like she doesn't fit in her own body," one tech had noted. The staff physician, Dr. Milland, had ordered a battery of neurological tests, but as far as David knew, none of them had yet shown any organic problem.

Beth settled into the chair, folding her hands in her lap and looking calmly at David.

"How are you?" he asked.

Her expression didn't change. "I have been informed that I am mentally ill," she replied. She had a low, rich voice, a "whiskey" voice like Lauren Bacall. "I find that surprising."

"Why do you find it surprising?" David asked.

"I was unaware that seeking asylum is the act of someone suffering from a deranged mind," Beth replied as if it were obvious.

"Asylum?" David asked.

Now she looked puzzled. "Of course. That is what the sign outside this building says: 'County Asylum.' It seems obvious that is where I would go when seeking such."

David Rosenberg had learned a long time ago not to laugh at a patient, but Beth was so...so quietly indignant...that he had to pause and wrestle his expression back to one of calm interest.

"I understand your confusion," he said at last. "You see, asylum has more than one meaning. It can mean a place of refuge or a place where one goes for treatment of mental and emotional problems." A sudden thought struck him.

"Is English your second language?" he asked delicately. *If she's an illegal, that would explain a lot, including why she won't give us her real name.*

Beth went white, the blood draining from her face so quickly that Dr. Rosenberg jumped to his feet and hurried around the desk, slipping a hand beneath her elbow in order to keep her from sliding out of the chair. He could feel the tremors running though her.

"It's all right," he said soothingly. "No one's going to turn you away; I promise. Whatever your status, you can stay here if you wish."

She pulled herself together quickly, her breathing evening out and a touch of color returning to the dead-white skin.

"Thank you," she murmured at last. "I am grateful for your consideration because right now, I have nowhere else to go."

"And you...aren't local, are you?" David made himself ask. She looked up at him, a strange expression in those sea-gray eyes.

"No," she replied slowly. "I am not, as you say, local."

"Okay." David took his seat once more and regarded his patient. She sat quietly as before, seemingly content to say nothing and allow him his thoughts.

"You came to us because you are in danger; is that right?" he asked at last. Beth simply nodded, and he waited for a few moments to see if she would elaborate on that answer, but she said nothing.

"All right," the doctor said at last. "While you are here, Beth, I would like to meet with you each day, perhaps at this time every afternoon. Would that be agreeable to you?"

She looked faintly surprised. "Why would it not be?" she

asked.

"Good," David replied, pleased. "We will meet and talk each day, and perhaps I can help you with...with whoever is threatening you." *Or better yet, perhaps we can fix your brain's chemical imbalance so you're no longer suffering these delusions.*

She shook her head. "No." Her voice was both sad and certain. "You cannot help me with my pursuers. But I will speak with you as you wish."

And that seemed as good a place as any to stop for the day. David sent her back to the ward and then pulled her chart to add a notation.

'Patient's paranoia still evident. She exhibits some of the behaviors and thought processes of a political prisoner. It is possible that she has escaped from a hostile regime; however, her country of origin has not yet been ascertained.'

"You're awfully quiet tonight," Michael Rosenberg observed one warm evening about ten days later.

David looked up from his veal picata and gave his husband an apologetic smile and shrug. "Yeah, I guess I am," he replied.

"A tough patient?" David often shared bits and pieces of his work with his mate, always being careful of course to preserve confidentiality. That wasn't a problem; Michael was a civil liberties lawyer and knew all about clients' rights.

"No," David replied slowly. "She's quite easy to work with--no drug addiction, no outbursts, doesn't seem to be a threat to herself or others. She's clinically depressed--I think-- and she's paranoid to an unusual degree for anyone not on drugs, but she seems..."

"Seems?" Michael prompted gently.

"Seems...like a princess in exile." The phrase slipped out without conscious thought, but even as he chuckled ruefully, David realized that he meant exactly what he'd just said.

Michael chuckled as well. "Anastasia lives, huh?" Both he and David were old movie buffs, and Ingrid Berman's portrayal of the lost Russian princess was one of their favorite films.

"About 90 years too late for that," David replied. "But there is something about her. I've met with her nine times now, but I can't seem to get anywhere. She won't talk about herself, her family, her past, anything. She just sits quietly, sips the cocoa I've been serving her in an effort to get some calories in her, and nods or shakes her head in response to most of my questions. Almost the only subject she will discuss is the fact that 'they' will kill her if they find her."

Michael was silent for a moment. "Is it possible that she's telling the truth?" he asked quietly.

David sighed. "Anything's possible, Mic; you know that. She could have escaped from one of the Balkan states; she's got that sort of Slavic peasant look. Maybe she was forced to be a drug mule; maybe someone kidnapped her as a child and pimped her out. I don't know, and she's not telling."

"I've got contacts at Amnesty International; we can put her into the database," Michael offered.

David shook his head decisively. "No, not without her knowledge and consent."

"Which she won't give you," Michael pointed out gently. David sighed, feeling the dull headache that he'd been nursing all day return.

"Which she won't give me," he agreed. "And I can't really blame her—if she truly is in danger there's no reason to trust me simply because I say so."

"What are you going to do?"

David sighed again. "What I always do—keep trying."

"I know you will." Michael got up from the table and came around to kiss the top of his mate's head. "How about some ice cream?" he suggested. "No reason to be frustrated and chocolate-deprived."

"No," David chuckled, good humor restored. "No reason at all."

"Why do you keep inviting me here?" Beth was seated in the chair she always chose, hands folded in her lap as always.

But at least today, she was actually talking. David felt the faintest flickering of hope.

"I ask you here to talk because I want to help you," he replied, putting as much sincerity in his tone and gaze as possible. But she shook her head.

"No." Her voice was certain and sad. "You wish to convince me that my fears are groundless, that I am mentally unbalanced."

"All right," he said gently. "Assuming that is true, is that such a bad thing?"

"If my fears were groundless, no," Beth told him. "But I can assure you, I am in danger." She fell silent, hands twisting together on her lap as she looked down at them. David was silent as well, hoping that given time and space, she might say more. But Beth was once again mute.

"If what you say is true," he said at last, feeling his way carefully, "then there should be some proof. And if there is proof, I will do all I can to make sure you are protected to the fullest extent of the law." At that, she looked up, grey eyes tearless but filled with such pain that David caught his breath, feeling a sudden twinge go through him.

"You cannot protect me," she said softly. "Only anonymity and perhaps sheer luck can do that. I must hope that they do not know where to look, for if they do find me, no law and no protection will be enough to save me."

He couldn't doubt her—or at least he couldn't doubt that she believed every word she said. It was written on her face like the lines of print on a page. David leaned forward.

"Beth, if you won't tell me who they are, can you at least tell me where they are?" he asked. "Are they here in America?"

Slowly, she shook her head. "I do not believe so," she replied in a low voice. "Indeed, they are probably not on this planet at all—at least, not yet." She glanced up as David's grandfather clock, a gift from Michael on their first anniversary, began to chime the hour. "I see our time is ended." Beth got to her feet, moving carefully as always.

"Until tomorrow, Dr. Rosenberg." With that, she let herself out, leaving David sitting at his desk and staring after her.

"You want me to believe you're being hunted by aliens."

It was two days later. David had been forced to cancel their regular appointment the previous day; one of his other patients had attempted suicide, and he'd spent much of the day dealing with the patient's family and arranging for more secure confinement in order to hopefully avert another near-disaster. Now, however, he could concentrate on Beth.

"I do not want you to believe anything," she replied calmly. "I told you the truth, doctor—at least, a piece of it. I realize that to you it sounds absurd. It is why I do not talk about my fears; I know many humans do not believe in extraterrestrial life."

"Many...humans?" David stared at her. "Are you saying that you're also an alien?"

"Yes." Her shoulders relaxed a fraction and she sighed. "That is exactly what I'm saying, Dr. Rosenberg. I am not native to this world, any more than are those who pursue me."

David felt his pulse leap with excitement. If he could disprove part of her delusions, perhaps the rest would follow. "Beth," he said, keeping his tone matter-of-fact, "I and the other doctors have examined you more than once." Now he smiled. "Believe me, I know a human being when I see one."

She simply gave him a look, the look of a mother disappointed by a bright child's inability to solve a puzzle. "Dr. Rosenberg, do you honestly think that if I am what I say I am, I am incapable of fooling human medical instruments? It's not difficult. Like most humans, you and the other medical staff see what you expect to see."

David thought quickly. If forced to face the unreality of her statements, Beth might crumble—but maybe such a crack would give him a way in to help her.

"All right," he said, keeping his voice calm. "If you are of extraterrestrial origin, prove it."

Beth gave him a long, considering look. "How do I know I won't end up in a cage somewhere on a top secret base in Nevada?" she asked.

David chuckled despite himself. "You've been watching X-Files reruns," he said. "You don't have to worry; I don't even know anyone from the FBI. Besides," he said more seriously, "you are my patient. Anything you reveal to me is confidential, Beth; you're smart enough to know that. And if you like, I will give you my personal word of honor that I won't share anything that happens in here, not even with the other doctors, unless you are dangerous to yourself or others."

For perhaps a minute, she simply studied him, those penetrating gray eyes seeming to look right down to his marrow. Then Beth nodded.

"Very well," she said, a faint smile on her lips. "Perhaps it will be easier if you know." She leaned back in the chair and closed her eyes for just a moment...

And then it happened. There was a faint shimmer, almost like the haze one sees on a blacktop road on a scorching August day. When it cleared, whatever was sitting in the good doctor's chair was nothing he'd seen before. It was humanoid, and it had Beth's clear gray eyes—but it had four of them, two in front, and one on each side of the head like a parrot fish. This being was much taller than Beth, perhaps seven feet, although it was hard to tell with it seated. Its head was completely hairless, and it had two holes where nostrils would be but no nose. It also had four arms, not two, each moving independently of the other.

David started, his gut clenching as his mind tried to convince his eyes they weren't seeing what they were looking right at. Beth held the pose, so to speak, for perhaps a dozen breaths, and then as quickly as she'd changed, she changed back to an ordinary-looking woman in pale blue sweats.

"Well," Beth said calmly, getting out of the chair, "perhaps we should break for today, doctor. I imagine you need some quiet time." She moved clumsily but swiftly out of the room, leaving David at his desk, head still spinning.

"Hey." Michael dropped down on the sofa next to David, putting an arm around his shoulders. "You seem preoccupied tonight," he said gently. "Most nights lately, in fact. Anything you want to talk about?"

David sighed and laid aside the journal he'd been re-reading for the last half-hour. "Nothing I can really talk about," he said regretfully.

"Your mystery patient?"

David nodded. "She's—well, like I said, I can't really discuss it. But she seems so...so plausible. I just don't know what to think. And there's....well, there's more, but that part I really can't talk about." He gave a small laugh. "I don't want you calling the white coats to haul me away."

Michael gave him a look of pure curiosity, but he knew the boundaries as well as David did when it came to patients, so he merely shrugged. "Well, your instincts are good, lover. I guess I'd have to tell you to trust your gut." He ran his hand up and down David's neck. "How about a massage?" he suggested. David turned and wrapped his arms around his partner, grateful once more for the kind fates that had given him this man.

"I want to know how you did that."

It was their appointment time the following day, and David leaned forward, almost glaring at his most perplexing patient. He'd barely slept at all the previous night, spending most of it pacing the floor, his mind replaying that extraordinary moment over and over again, trying to figure out how it had happened like a kid watching a magician's trick through a hundred shows.

At dawn, he still didn't know.

"How did you pull off that trick?"

"It wasn't a trick," Beth replied tiredly. "That is my true appearance. This..." she gestured to herself, "is a trick." She sighed. "But I knew that my demonstration would not satisfy you. So, what more proof do you want?"

David felt as if he were quickly losing control of the discussion. "Look, you don't have to…"

"No, I do," she replied, almost angry now. She looked around. "Do you have anything sharp?"

David paled.

"Oh, don't be ridiculous," Beth said impatiently. "I'm not going to cut my wrists. Have you got a penknife or even a needle?"

Actually, David did have a needle and thread in his desk drawer. He was famous for pulling the buttons off of his jackets when he yanked them off and rolled up his sleeves in hot weather, so Michael had finally persuaded him to learn how to sew a button back on when needed. He reached in the drawer and withdrew the needle. David hesitated for another moment, wondering if Beth would do something extreme, like drive the needle into her eye. She must have picked up on his concerns, because she stood up and moved closer to the desk, holding out one finger.

"Go ahead."

Feeling like he was humoring a madwoman (and frankly, he probably was), David nonetheless carefully and deliberately plunged the needle into the offered finger. Beth didn't flinch. He pulled the needle out…and watched as first one then several drops of bright purple blood beaded up on her skin. Beth grabbed a Kleenex from the box on his desk and wadding it up held it against her finger for a few moments until the bleeding stopped. She then handed the tissue to David.

"It's….it's purple," he said stupidly.

"Indeed," Beth replied, re-seating herself. "I'm not sure why it is that color; I suspect there are some rare trace minerals in my blood that react with the hemoglobin to produce that hue, but obviously I do not have access to a lab to find out." She looked at David. "I suspect, however, that you do," she continued. "Feel free to have my blood analyzed. I ask only that you keep my identity secret as you agreed."

It wasn't blood.

At least, that's what the lab results claimed. David stared at the paper, translating the lab's drawn-out phrases and hedging into real-people speak. Once all the technical terms were weeded out, the final answer was something along the lines of, "We don't know what this substance is, and quit trying to jerk us around; this isn't April 1st."

There was a knock on his office door, and David thrust the paper into the drawer and looked up as Beth came in, walking as always with that peculiar gait, as if she wasn't comfortable in her own body. She made her way to the chair and sat down.

"You miss the extra limbs."

Startled, she looked at him.

"It's why you seem....well, clumsy," David said apologetically. "You're used to having those extra two arms for balance."

The color drained from her face as she absorbed the meaning of his statement. "Yes," she almost whispered. "That and the eyes; I do not understand how you humans can manage with such crippled peripheral vision. I constantly fear I will bump into or fall over an object I do not perceive in time. You...you believe me now."

David spread his hands in the classic palms-up gesture of helplessness. "I can't do anything else," he replied. "Even assuming I was hallucinating when you shape-shifted, that blood work was pretty conclusively not human. But I don't understand any of this. Why are you here on Earth? Why are you in danger? Do your....people know about Earth, about us?"

"My people know a hundred and yet another hundred worlds like Earth," Beth said softly. "The universe is far more populated than you humans believe—curious because you have such rich literature and dramatic presentations on the subject, and you have sent so many probes out looking for life in other places—and yet never expected to find it." She gave him a small but genuine smile. "Now you have."

"But why are you here?"

She sighed. "Because, as I told you, I am in danger. On my world, there is an oppressive government that is slowly draining the life from our people, crushing them with burdens of taxation and tribute, enslaving those who cannot pay, killing those who protest. I am one of those, a leader among my people. My identity was compromised by a traitor to our group, and those who rule us now know who I am—and if they find me, they will kill me. Off-planet was my only choice, and my only chance. I have to be somewhere they will not think to look—and they will think of a great many places. A hospital on this small, out-of-the-way world seemed ideal."

"And you expect me to believe that you are some kind of interstellar freedom fighter," David said.

Beth shrugged. "I have no way to prove my words, unless they find me," she replied quietly. "For your sake and the sake of those here, I must pray that day never comes."

It was a rainy Thursday evening. After a dinner of David's favorite honey mustard chicken and wild rice, followed by one of Michael's truly exceptional chocolate soufflés, the two had curled up on the couch, Michael going over some papers and David half-heartedly flipping through a copy of Psychology Today. At last he set it down on the coffee table and yawned.

"I'm wiped," he said. "I'm going to turn in, okay?"

His partner nodded. "Sure thing; I'll be done with this in about an hour, and I'll join you," he said.

David leaned over and gave him a quick kiss. "It's a date," he murmured playfully.

The sudden shrill dinging of David's emergency pager put paid to those plans.

"What the Hell happened here?" David ran into Beth's room, right into the knot of med-tech gathered around her on the floor. One look, and he didn't need to ask what had happened. Somehow, she'd managed to obtain a pair of nylons and had looped them around her neck, climbing on a chair and attaching them to the window frame. David stood rooted to the floor, staring down at the still, gray features, as adrenalin and CPR were administered, as a half-dozen professionals fought Death—and lost. Ten minutes after David had arrived, the floor attending pronounced. Beth Doe was officially no longer a patient.

It was late. David had filled out all the necessary, mind-numbing, dreadful paperwork that a death on the ward required. He felt nothing, absolutely dead inside. In more than 20 years of practice, he'd only lost five to suicide—Beth was his sixth.

Maybe if I hadn't named her after my sister, he thought dully—but that way lay madness. He headed for the door, moving through the quiet ward. Most of the patients were asleep. He reached the door before he saw her.

"Doctor?"

David jumped as Joanne came out of the shadows, more cadaverous than ever. Despite weeks of therapy and medication, she was still starving herself and planning her own funeral pyre. "Joan, I didn't see you." She stopped just short of David, reaching out one bony hand to pat his sleeve.

"Don't feel bad," she said in that whispery, quavering voice of hers. "She knew they were coming for her, you see."

"What? Joan, what are you talking about?" Fatigue and stress made his voice snappish, but Joan didn't seem to notice.

"Here; I'll show you." She took hold of his sleeve and tugged until he followed her across the common room to the small pile of magazines donated by staff members. She burrowed in the pile until she found last week's Time Magazine, flipping it open to a page that was turned down at the corner.

"See?" She saw that after dinner tonight, and she told me

she'd have to go," Joan explained. "She knew they would be after her, so she shed this body and moved on. She said this place was not an asylum for her, not anymore."

Dully, David stared down at the article in the magazine's Science section. The headline read, "New Comet Coming Close to Earth on the 26th." The 26th was the next day.

"Oh, no," David moaned softly. "Oh, Beth, no...."

His phone rang, and he wearily picked up the receiver. It was the morgue, located in the hospital's basement.

"Doc," the attendant said, "you need to get down here—now."

David stared down at the stainless slab that the attendant had pulled from its drawer. There was no body—only a vaguely human-shaped mound of ashes.

"What happened?"

The morgue attendant shrugged. "Hell if I know," he replied. "I came in and I could smell it, like a hot grill after a cookout. I checked all the drawers and there she was—ashes, like one of those old cases of spontaneous combustion you read about in Ripley's Believe It or Not. I swear, Doc, I didn't do anything."

"No," David said quietly. "I'm sure you didn't." He looked at the man, reading the tag on his uniform.

"Look—Chad," he said. "I can launch an investigation, have every orderly and nurse interviewed, but what difference will it make? She...as far as I know, there's no family. She would have been cremated anyway." He forced a sick and sour smile. "I guess it's been done for us. Put on a contamination suit and transfer the remains to a container. I'll take care of the paperwork."

Chad looked relieved. "Thanks Doc." He shivered slightly. "I've worked here for six years; I've seen a lot. But this—this is fucking creepy."

"Yeah." Creepier than you know, David thought, but at least this would save Beth from an X-Files-style autopsy.

It was the end of a very long day. David hadn't felt that he could cancel his sessions with other patients; they still needed him, but he hadn't been at his best this day, and he knew it. He leaned back and his chair and closed his tired, burning eyes, trying to get up the strength to switch off his desk lamp and go home. Beth was in the cold room in the hospital's basement. Tomorrow he'd have to see about filing the paperwork so he could claim her remains and give her a decent burial. He owed her that much; it was far less than he should have done. There should have been some way to reach her, some way to keep her from that final, fatal act. If only I'd been able to reach her...

There was a knock on the door, and David sat up, feeling about a million years old. "Come in," he called, sounding as defeated as he felt. The door opened. It was Nurse Van Camp with a tall slender gentleman in a blue suit at her right shoulder.

"Dr. Rosenberg," she said. "This gentleman has come about Beth."

David got to his feet at once, confused. "But..." He stopped just short of saying, "But she didn't know anyone here on Earth." Instead, he pulled his professional mask over his features and nodded. He stepped around the desk to shake the pale, slim hand offered to him.

"Thank you, Nurse." David indicated a chair. "Won't you sit down, Mr....."

"Smith," the gentleman said agreeably. He took the chair, the same one Beth had sat in so often, and David nodded to the nurse. "Thank you, Ms. Van Camp. You may go." He waited until the door had closed. So did his visitor.

"So," David said at last, "Who are you going to try to convince me you are? A boyfriend? A cousin?"

His visitor shook his head.

"No," he replied simply. "She told you, did she not? I thought so. When I touched your hand, you projected rather loudly, Ailien told you of her real identity, or at least a part of it."

"Ailien," David repeated. "That...was her name?"

"Yes," the man—only, he probably wasn't a man—replied. "I have been looking for her for several months." David's lips tightened.

"She told me she was being pursued," David said with quiet bitterness. "I didn't believe her, not really. I should have." He looked at the quiet man across the desk. "Now what? Do you kill me too, or just wipe my mind clean? She's dead; why are you even here? You got what you want. She's no threat to you and your thugs anymore!"

The man leaned forward. "Doctor, please calm yourself," he said gently. "I am no threat to you. I do not intend to harm you in any way. Ailien was right; I was pursuing her, but not for the reasons she undoubtedly told you. I am a pash'uka, a mind-healer for my people, just as you are for yours. Ailien escaped confinement from the facility where her family had sent her. She was suffering from...well, I believe the closest human equivalent is paranoid schizophrenia." The quiet man shook his head regretfully. "It's such a pity. She was so young—barely more than an adolescent by our standards. I had so hoped I could reach her, save her from this end." He got this feet.

"I will not disturb you further," he said kindly. "I plan to stay on this planet for a few days; would it be possible for me to get Ailien's ashes? I believe her family would be comforted if I can bring her home."

David nodded slowly. "Yeah," he said at last. "I'll fill out the forms, and I'll let you know as soon as her remains are released." He took one of his cards from the desk and handed it to the man. "You can contact me here—if you know how to use a phone."

A slight smile flickered across the melancholy features. "I will figure it out, as you say." The quiet man replaced his hat, bowed his head slightly and turned towards the door. Then he turned back.

"I grieve with you, doctor," he said softly. "We both lost a patient." He slipped out, leaving David sitting at his desk as the shadows gathered and the room grew chill.

Edited by Sam Taylor

WHERE DID WE COME FROM?

By Steve Guest

Dad?

Yeah mate?

Where did we come from?

Our mums mate.

No, I mean all of us. People.

Earth mate.

Earth's a planet isn't it?

Yep, that's Earth, just there. We used to live there you know.

What? You, me and mum?

No, no. We, as in Humans we.

Really? When?

Oh about three thousand years ago.

Why don't we live there now? Does anyone still live there?

Oh no lad. No one could live there. It is what you call sterile. Not even the hardiest bacteria, or bugs could survive in the 'illudium' field.

What's an illudium field dad?

Well, mate, illudium was a particle or tiny little dot, smaller than the eye can see, that was produced at a place called Europe in a monstorously large machine called a collider. It smashes tiny bits of stuff called 'matter' together, at speeds fast enough to travel from here to gramar's house and back twenty times in a second.

That's pretty slow.

Yeah, anyway, when these particles hit each other at those speeds, they smash apart to reveal their smaller bits. But a clever man realised that if you put the right type of particles, or bits of matter in and applied enough magnetism and speed you could get them to start a reaction of matter nearby, that kept on giving off energy, or power many times that of what was needed for the thing to get going.

So this very clever man, did just that. The stuff that was produced was called 'illudium' and it caused anything near it to convert to illudium as well, and as it did, it let off a formidable amount of power in the form of light, things called gamma and x radiation, heat and also had the effect of clumping together. As it became clumpier, the little bits called electrons and protons were pushed off leaving just things called neutrons in the clump. Now when I say clump, it actually is the closest thing to perfectly round that you can imagine, and packed so tightly by the process that it is billions of times heavier than anything of its size. Now when things become that heavy or massive as it is known, they have more gravity, or 'pull' on other things. This action, or reaction as it were, started to pull and convert everything, and it grew and grew as it literally devoured everything bit by bit. There was no stopping it.

So how did people get away?

They didn't.

So how are we here then?

Well, there was a program set up by our ancestors back then to explore and colonise this very planet. The country was called China, and with the help of a few of the other countries, set about to 'terraform' as well as explore here. Terraforming is making a planet habitable or liveable for humans and other species by making sure that liquid water and air is available.

How did they do that here dad?

Algae and cold fusion Billy. Algae and good old cold fusion.

When your great great great etc. etc. granpa got here with the sixty other scientists, engineers, technitions, doctors and such, the first thing they did was set up a heater plant like the one that keeps us warm in the Darkening, at the poles of our planet. It took three years for water to start running. There was an unimaginable amount in the surface, and with it came dormant or sleeping bugs from deep down, that needed very little nutrient and even less air. In fact the clever little things could use the hydrogen in water to survive and prosper. Any form of energy, like light, heat or strong enough radio waves, was enough to allow them to convert the water into stuff to survive on.

Now they were an amazing and fortunate bonus for two very important reasons. Firstly, they poo out oxygen, and pee out carbon and nitrogen; and secondly, they form a set of very complex protein amino acidy stuff, like in meat, when they get into an acidy environment like our tummies and insides, and when they die after reproducing or making copies of themselves, our bodies absorb them and we get a free feed.

Now alone, these little buggers would have taken many thousands of years to produce an atmosphere here, but with the algae brought from earth, the process was very quick. Within three generations, we had plants started, within another two generations a rich topsoil was starting to form. From there it was just time and some more development of ideas and techniques and we had grasses and soils, trees and best of all; these little fellas, built right out of the genetic containers they arrived in.

"Binny! Come here boy." Dad, did all of the animals come from jinotic containers?

That's genetic, mate, and yes. Lucky some foresighted scientist knew the value of seeding genetic material on a barren planet. You can see the big cube of a container at the settlement museum that housed all of the genetic material for all of the animals, both male and female genes. The container is called Noah's Ark. I guess that the scientist in charge must have been called Noah, and 'ark' is an old term for box.

Why is Earth so bright in the sky dad?

It's a pure neutron planet and everything that gets drawn toward it glows as it is converted to illudium.

Dad, did someone make all the stars and planets and everything else?

Nah mate. But stupid people back on Earth used to think that some bloke named Gord or Gawd, or God or something like that, did.

None of the settlers were allowed to come here if they were foolish enough to believed in anything unscientific.

Dad?

Yes mate?

Why did they disassemble uncle Ming?

He hurt someone mate.

I miss him.

Yeah, me too. But he hurt someone mate. Had to be done.

Yeah, I suppose.

Dad?

Yeah mate?

Can me and Xin go to Jupiter for a look?

Yeah mate, but be back by five, and stay away from Earth, ok.

Yeah dad, ok.

See ya.

See ya mate. Hey! Do up your Norden, and think your mum before you go. You know what she's like.

Ok. Bye...

ROBBY

By Debbie Painter

Knock, knock, knock. A moment of silence. Knock! Knock! Knock!

The young woman looked around her, frowning slightly. She had heard and seen no one, but there appeared to be signs of life around the old abandoned house. The cicadas, excited by her pounding, began to grind out their peculiar pee-ahh-pee-ahh, blanking out any other sound she might have heard, and Sherry Hayes put her long hand on an ample hip.

Knock, knock, knock. "Child welfare," she called, her frustration evident. "Please open the door. I only need to speak with you."

For a brief moment, she had the feeling that she had done this before. Looking around her, the high grass and brush, the overgrown yard, and the entire place seemed to be a memory. Yet she knew she had never been here. She knew the place by reputation only. Her old-fashioned parents had made certain that she had not hung out here with her peers when she was of that age.

Nothing. That feeling of déjà vu ended, and she felt the same as she had before. Hot, sweaty, and annoyed. She stepped away from the door, looking longingly at her nearby vehicle and its air conditioning. It must be 100 degrees, she estimated, and she felt like she was melting in the steamy summer air. The relief air conditioning could bring was so tempting, but no, not yet, she decided. It was too soon to give up. She could take a look around the old house. Maybe she could find someone here.

Stepping gingerly off the aged porch, she looked at the old, decrepit house. Part of the porch had collapsed in on itself, and the kids from the community had long ago knocked out every one of the glass windows. Coming here and doing so had bestowed a certain amount of youthful swagger to several generations of the community's teens. The place looked to be one lost nail away from total collapse, and the yard was totally overgrown with weeds, brush, and even sizable trees. No one had lived here during her lifetime, she recalled. Built before the new highway had gone through, it stood half a mile or so off the nearest road, but that was not what had kept people away from it. This was a murder house, and folks here about tended to avoid places with a reputation such as that. Granted, the double murder had occurred when her mother was a girl, but no one in the county would go near the old Williams house after that.

So what was a child doing living here alone? Sherry had two referrals from people in the community expressing their concern about a child living here, apparently untended. No one had been able to get near the child who skittered away when approached. She had come as soon as the case was assigned, but no one she had been able to locate in the neighborhood could give her any additional information, leaving her only to enter the long-abandoned property alone in search of an unfortunate child.

She pulled out her phone. Quickly punching in a number, she waited until someone picked up on the other end. "Margaret? Yes, this is Sherry. I'm out here at the old Williams house on that referral you gave me and I haven't found anyone. No, there is some evidence of someone being here so I'm going to keep looking. I should be back at the office in, say, forty-five minutes unless I find something. OK, see you then."

It never hurt to check in with the office, she reasoned, especially when the investigation was occurring in a place as isolated as this. As a child protection specialist, Sherry was accustomed to being in odd places with even stranger people, but this place set her nerves to jangling. Something was not right. But if there had been anyone around they were not here now, she concluded as she walked around the overgrown yard, a stick in her hand in case she had to drive off a snake. This place was rattlesnake heaven if she had ever seen it.

She'd come back later with a police officer, she concluded. The county guys were always glad to go on an easy run, they said, so she didn't expect much resistance if she asked for an escort when she tried to get into the house. Looking down at her best skirt and blouse, she shook her head. She definitely needed to change clothes for what she needed to do next. Fortunately, she kept a spare set of jeans and a shirt in the car just for moments like this. Too many of her nicer things had been ruined before she learned the lesson that jumping creeks and chasing kids down the street were not duties in which she should wear her best clothes.

Sliding into her small SUV, Sherry sighed as she put the A/C on maximum, did a neat three-point turn, and returned down the overgrown drive. The long-untended grounds had become so overgrown that the undergrowth easily reached higher than her head in places, making her feel enclosed and slightly claustrophobic. The driveway was a tunnel over which massive old oaks and maples towered cutting off the sunlight, and the weeds and brush grew into the road, almost obscuring it in places. How could a child have found this place, much less have chosen it for a home? It was unlikely, she knew, but she had heard and seen worse.

Then she saw it. Something at the edge of her vision. Something that looked like a child according to its size, but she had not gotten a sufficient look to know for sure. Slamming on the brakes, Sherry put the vehicle in park and threw open the door. Rolling out quickly, she darted back up the drive and searched the patch of underbrush where she thought she had seen a human figure. If the child had been there, he or she was there no longer. Even the dry grasses bore no mark of a human foot. Strange, she thought, she had been so certain.

Returning to the vehicle, she grabbed her phone and punched in the number for the county sheriff's department. She couldn't leave now, of course. Whatever this was, she had seen it, too.

Larry Giles answered. She had worked with him before and liked the tall, angular evangelical convert. His earnestness and calm demeanor always earned points with her.

"Larry, this is Sherry Hayes."

"I'm thinking this is not a pleasure call, Sherry," he drawled. "What can I do for you?"

"I'm out here at the old Williams place."

He whistled. "Why on earth are you there? Nobody's lived in that place for years."

"That's the problem, Larry. I've had two referrals that there is a kid out here, and I just saw something myself. Whatever I saw is quick and elusive. I need some backup to help me search the place. There's signs of occupation around the house, and I just saw something as I was going out the driveway."

She could almost hear the calm, methodical gears turning in Larry Giles' head. "I can cut myself free," he said almost immediately. "I think I can get one or two of the boys to come with me. It's near shift change, but if there's an abandoned kid out there I don't think the boss is going to mind a little bit of overtime. I'll clear it with him and we should be there in, say, twenty minutes."

"All right," she agreed. "I'll see who I can shake loose at my place. I'm going to stay here in the drive where I've seen the kid until I get some backup. This place is going to be a bitch to search, but there is definitely something here, Larry."

"Hey, honey," he quipped, "if there is anybody over there at your place that can handle this, it's you, Sherry."

She laughed a hearty, deep belly laugh. "Larry, you are so full of it. You keep talking like that and I'll have to speak with your sweet wife."

He laughed brightly at that. "See ya in twenty, sweetie."

"I'll be right here."

She had no luck at her office although she was not surprised. Many days passed when its lone occupant was their stolid, unflappable secretary, Mary Lou. The ancient secretary, Sherry suspected, must have been present eons ago when the department had been formed because Mary Lou knew every administrator within the department and was a particularly favorite employee of the governor. Her longevity was legendary, and even though she did less and less, passing on many responsibilities to younger women, no one had the heart to tell her that she must leave. After fifty years or so, Mary Lou had become the department in this county and she would leave when she chose to leave, probably toes up.

"Sorry, darling," Mary Lou said when Sherry called asking for help. "We're plumb out of help today. Reesie is over at the school on a possible sex abuse case, Richard is moving a kid to the west end of the state, and Rosie is out at the hospital on a suspected abuse."

"What about Margaret?" Sherry asked.

Mary Lou chuckled heartily. "Well, darlin'you know Miss Margaret doesn't really like to get her hands dirty."

The remark hung in the air, acknowledged by them both as annoying and truthful. Margaret's appointment was political, they all knew. She came from a prominent family and was well placed socially. There had been no position when Margaret had decided that she wanted to take up social work, but a position had quickly been created for her. However, generally what that meant was Margaret worked at what she chose to do and did not work otherwise. No, Mary Lou was right, Sherry knew. Margaret would not want to come out here and beat through the brush trying to find a missing child. She might find herself someway inconvenienced.

"Don't worry about it, Mary Lou. I'm not positive there's anyone out here, but the county is sending some guys to help me check the property. I thought I saw something, too."

"You be careful, darlin," the ancient secretary drawled. "If you decide you need somebody else, call and I'll come. Margaret can answer the damned phones for a while. 'N' I'll bring my pistol, too, darlin'. I think this notion of you gals not going armed is the stupidest thing I ever heard."

"Sure thing. I'll let you know what we find." She smiled at Mary Lou's words. Yes, Mary Lou would certainly come out here and come armed if she thought that anyone was threatening or endangering her 'girls' as she called the staff. Her protectiveness was charming, especially considering her physical frailty.

Sherry had taken about three months on the job to figure out how this system worked. Every office and job had its own flow, and Mary Lou was very much at the heart of theirs. She was secretary, chief cheerleader, receptionist, babysitter, and occasional forager when a child came into custody in the middle of the night and no clothes were to be had. How that old woman managed to place a few calls and come up with what they needed almost every time was beyond Sherry, but it was not beyond Mary Lou. What they would do to replace her when the time came – and they all knew it was coming – Sherry did not know.

She eyed the jeans and t-shirt once more and decided if she was going to undress in the middle of all this underbrush she had best do it before her team arrived. Growing up country had meant that she had shed clothes in the open air to change into bathing suits or go skinny dipping before, and she slipped out of her good clothes with a skill that showed long practice, folding them carefully and putting them out of harm's way. The jeans and t-shirt slid on like her skin, and within moments her sneakers and socks completed the outfit, customary rubber bands around the bottoms of the legs to keep out bugs and other unpleasant critters that might hide in the deep brush. In order to be turned in the right direction, she started her car and had just managed to do a second three point turn in the narrow, overgrown landscape when her police escort arrived. Reluctantly, she stepped out of the car with its blessed air conditioning to greet her team.

Waving to her, Larry Giles pulled the aging Crown Vic issued him by the county to a halt and exited the vehicle, leaving it running. Behind him, another cruiser stopped and its inhabitants, George Smith and Howard Frances, joined them. Larry's easy, calm manner was always a plus when dealing with the younger and less experienced men, and Sherry hoped that everything would go smoothly. In a few sentences, she was able to tell them why she had come and what she had observed. Larry surveyed the landscape before coming to a conclusion.

"I know you think you saw something down here, Sherry," he said, "but let's go back to the house to look. There is so much underbrush here and we could look all day and not find something right under our feet. You said earlier that there were some tracks around the house, right?"

She nodded. "I'm all right with that. I've been here since I called and haven't seen or heard a thing. Whatever it was that I saw is gone."

"Then let's move up to the house."

Within five minutes, the four of them were standing on what had once been the front lawn of the old Williams house. The roof had collapsed into the building, leaving a dark and cavernous hole. Mounds of rocks were strewn all around, a result of county boys showing their bravado by daring to break the windows. All the ancient structure needed to be complete was a Boo Radley to act as the resident mad man. As they looked for an entrance, the front door surrounded by an overgrown rose garden with its multitude of thorns was quickly eliminated as an option by the team in favor of a small side door which was much more accessible.

George Smith took one step into the house and the floor collapsed under the weight of his foot. He swore violently and lurched away, almost managing to avoid a fall, but his oaths did not stop then. "Damn, damn, damn," he said again and again. "I think I broke my ankle."

The other two men lifted him up and half carried him to a relatively clear place in the yard where they could examine him. By the time they could get his shoe off, blood was welling up black under the skin.

"Damn," Larry Giles swore softly. "If you haven't broken

it, you've missed the best opportunity I've seen all day." He looked levelly at Howard Frances. "Go get the car and pull it up as close as you can. You need to take him on to the hospital before this really starts to hurt because it's gonna hurt like a son-of-a-bitch here in a little while."

Howard nodded silently and turned toward the car. He was back in minutes, and when they had managed to load Smith into the car Howard drove away with his partner in the front seat still swearing a blue streak.

"I hope they make it to the hospital before that thing really starts to hurt," Larry said as they watched the other two men go.

"Me, too." Sherry turned to the house. "Larry, under the circumstances, I think we need to look outside unless there is some overwhelming indicator that someone is inside. The whole thing could come down on our heads if the flooring is that rotten."

"Just what I was thinking. Let me call the chief first." He pulled his radio, quickly notified his boss that they had an injured officer en route to the hospital, and let him know that they would only be searching outside at this point. Then he pointed in one direction and started off in the other by himself. Sherry chuckled affectionately. That was what she really liked about Larry. Not a lot of talk but plenty of action.

She had broken a path through the weeds and brush that was roughly a third of the way around the house when Sherry Hays thought she heard something again, a loud whistling sound that was almost mechanical. It was strange that she had not heard that before. After a moment, the sound died away and the only noise left was the chirping of the crickets and the call of the cicadas in the hot, late summer air. She took two more steps and heard another sound; something like gears. Again, when she paused, what she thought she had heard quit. Looking at her next step, she deliberately avoided the brush which had been knocking against her jeans, attempting to move as silently through the weeds and clutter as possible. One step, one step, one step.

The thing appeared so suddenly before her that she squealed despite her best efforts. It was small like a child but looked more mechanical than human. Its head, if that is what it could be called, swiveled on a narrow neck, and when it faced her a high-pitched squeal was emitted. A sequence of distressed sounding noises came rapidly in succession, and when Sherry realized the thing was about to bolt she grabbed.

Bad idea. Everything in her training said not to do this, but she knew if she did not take rapid action that the thing would flee her presence again. The funny thing was that as soon as she touched it, the squeals dissipated into the summer background noise and it remained in place. Instead, she could hear a low, rumbling noise. The sound was pleasant, satisfied.

She glanced up to see Larry Giles fifteen or twenty feet away, his service revolver pulled and his arm locked into position to fire.

"Don't, Larry," she said softly. "I think we're all right. Put the gun away but don't move closer. It seems to like me."

Unflappable Larry Giles swore softly and did not move. "What the hell is that thing?" he said softly, his pistol still at the ready.

"I'm not really sure, Larry, but if it wanted to hurt me it could already have done that. Please put your pistol away. I don't want you to frighten it."

"'Frighten it?'" Larry repeated in clear dismay. "Shit, Sherry, I nearly pissed my pants. What is it?"

She smiled in delicious irony. "I don't know exactly, Larry, but for the moment I'm going to make the assumption that this is young, whatever it is, and in need of protection. Sure can't leave it here."

"Please tell me that we are not going remove that thing, Sherry, and put it in state's custody," he almost whined. "We'll both be the laughing stock of our departments."

"Larry, if this is what I think it might be, we'll be famous all over the world for protecting it." She grinned saucily.

"Might be enough to get rid of Margaret. Maybe they'll give me her cushy job doing nothing."

"But that thing is not even human," Larry persisted.

Sherry smiled brilliantly. "It is small, child size. Do you see another one of these things around? You know, adult sized? Well, I don't either so I am assuming that this is a young, abandoned whatever. We're taking it to the office."

"Why does this surprise me?" Larry Giles muttered softly as he finally holstered his pistol. "I'm still getting ribbed over the rabbit thing."

Deciding to come back for the spare car, Larry drove Sherry's SUV once they had maneuvered the small being into it. There had been a certain degree of challenge to putting the robot, as Sherry had now started to think of it, with minimal leg length into an SUV and still be able to utilize the proper child restraints. Human child restraints were just not built for a being three to four feet in height with minimal leg length, and she held her breath with every creak of the over-stressed but required child restraint device. It may look ridiculous, but she was going to follow every law to the letter.

Before they arrived at the office, the little robot had begun to click in that way that Sherry thought previously meant distress, and she reached again to take an appendage, hoping to soothe the creature. Holding hands made it hum pleasantly so she continued that until Larry pulled her vehicle into the office parking lot.

"Would you go through the lobby to see if there's anyone there but Mary Lou?' she requested. "I think we need to keep this quiet."

Larry looked at her as though he couldn't believe what she had just said. "Quiet? Quiet, Sherry? What makes you think we have any chance of keeping this quiet? First time the TV stations hear about this, they'll be all over the story."

"Larry," she replied, her mood remarkably light, "this is a confidential matter and will be handled as such."

Larry nodded uncertainly and returned within a minute or two to say the path was clear. The only remaining task was getting the robot out of the child restraint device and back on a flat surface, not as simple, Sherry mused, as one might think. Hitting the warm asphalt, the robot chirped unhappily, she thought, and once more Sherry took its appendage and led the little machine forward.

"Oh, my sweet Lord," she heard Mary Lou say before the door had completely closed behind the three of them, cutting them off from the blistering summer heat. "Larry said you had something unusual but...Sherry, what is that?"

"This is what was out at the Williams place," Sherry responded smoothly, feeling a motherly protectiveness for her charge. "I have removed it and brought it into custody."

"Honey, that ain't a kid."

"Mary Lou, this is a small something with no obvious supervision. If it were a child, I would bring it into custody for its protection. Who are we to say that this...being...doesn't need our protection, too?"

"Honey, I think your trolley done jumped the track. Margaret is gonna shit."

There was that, of course. Margaret never wanted any unnecessary attention from anywhere. Attention might draw notice to her lack of action and initiative. Getting people to look at this office might actually require Margaret to do something. Sherry smiled maliciously. She hoped they got lots of attention over this little thing, whatever it was.

Now that they were in her territory, Sherry took her first long look at her small charge, circling it slowly. The little machine – and that is all that she could think it was – rose slightly higher than her waist with rollers for feet at the end of its short legs. It had a strange, round head. The torso was shaped slightly somewhat like a bullet and had very little shape otherwise. The little thing rotated its head backward at her gaze as though it was giving her the same, evaluating look. Sherry smiled despite herself. Whatever this thing was, she liked it.

Turning her eyes to Larry Giles, Sherry started to thank him for his help and send him on his way, but he shook his head as though he anticipated her thoughts.

"No way am I leaving you all with this," he drawled. "I'm not sure what it is, but I'm not leaving it in an office full of women and not a weapon between the three of you."

"I hardly think we need protection," Sherry chided gently.

"Until we know what that thing is and what it can do, I'm not leaving you. End of discussion." Larry's mouth set in that stubborn way he had when his mind was made up and nothing short of death was going to change it.

"Good," Sherry said, smiling despite herself. "Take it back to my office while I get the paperwork."

"Paperwork? What do you mean?"

"Can't do a removal without doing the paperwork, Larry. You've been around long enough to know that."

"But this thing isn't even human," he objected.

"We got it. We've got to document it."

As Sherry turned away, she didn't even need to see Larry's face to know that he was rolling his eyes in dismay. The ridiculousness of the situation made her grin broadly. She couldn't wait for Margaret to see this thing.

Larry and the little robot were in her office eyeing one another uncertainly when Sherry entered the room. The machine was making a low, chirping sound so she reached over briefly as she passed to run her hand over the slick metal head. That seemed to soothe the little thing and she perched at her desk, angled so that she could see both Larry and the small mechanism at the same time.

Sherry put the camera to her face to take the identifying photograph necessary for her file. The little machine began to squeak in an entirely new and uncertain way. As she clicked the button, the camera flashed and the small being squealed loudly, the portals she assumed were eyes blinking madly. She gave it another pat of reassurance and settled into her desk chair.

She looked up at Larry. "We're going to have to call it

126

something."

He grunted softly in dismay. "It's a thing, Sherry, a machine. It doesn't need a bloody name."

Flipping the paper around, she pointed to the top line."Name, date of birth, home address. It's gotta be filled out."

The officer did roll his eyes at her then, and Sherry pulled at her lower lip thoughtfully as she considered the question. "We've got an address. We can use the Williams place. That's no problem. But he doesn't seem to talk or anything so I guess we'll just have to name him."

"'Him'?" Larry echoed woodenly. "Why are you calling it him?"

Sherry laughed. It was a low, throaty sound. "A girl just knows these things, Larry."

"But what are you going to do about the rest? The name, date of birth. Hell, I know your paperwork well enough. You even need a bloody Social Security number, and I know he doesn't have one of those things." Then he realized what he'd done and snapped, "Christ, you've got me doing it, too, Sherry. Talking about this machine like he is a kid."

"How do you know it's not?"

That stumped the unflappable deputy. "But don't you think we should notify somebody? Someone official? We've found a functional robot, Sherry? Nobody's in control of it. Shouldn't somebody know about it? It's not like anyone's ever seen something like this before. Especially around here."

"Larry, you're a sheriff's deputy and I am a child protection investigator. Between your badge and my ID, there's not much of anywhere in this state we can't go except some of the national labs. We're about as official as it gets." She pushed the stack of uncompleted documents around in front of her before looking up at him. "Who are we going to notify if we were going to do it anyway? There's not exactly a Department of Lost Child Robots around here, is there?"

He was angry, she could see, and Sherry regretted that. If

she had been completely honest, she would have confessed that she was really flying by the seat of her pants on this anyway. She didn't know what to do. She was making it up as she went along because there was sure as hell no protocol in her rule books for putting a baby robot into foster care. Until she saw the thing, she hadn't even thought something like that existed, but clearly it did. The proof of its existence stood on the floor before her whirring slightly as its gears shifted and interlocked.

"OK, since it can't tell us anything," she finally said, "I'm going to name this thing. It's now Robby Robot until we come up with a better name."

"That's not very original."

"Can you do better?" she snapped. Larry fell quiet, and there was a long, awkward silence before Sherry picked up a pen and began to complete the myriad forms necessary to document what she had just done, copying the name she had just given the robot, the address of the old Williams place, using the current day's date as date of birth, and a workaround Social Security number on each and every separate form.

Once she had made those decisions and established them as basic facts, completing the paperwork was a matter of rote. There were, of course, no parent signatures or notices, and it was only when she skipped those time after time did she stop to wonder how Robby had come to be out at the Williams place completely alone. Maybe robots didn't have parents, but there had to be someone or something around, didn't there? Robby hadn't just popped into existence on his own.

About the time she was finishing the inch or two of paperwork on her removal of the little robot, Sherry heard the backdoor slam and knew that it must be Margaret. Mary Lou had been holding down the fort in the reception area while Sherry had completed the forty or fifty pieces of paper needed to justify her work. Yes, the newcomer would be Margaret. Sherry smiled broadly. Margaret's reaction was about to make her day.

As the footsteps proceeded down the hall past her door, Sherry called loudly, "Margaret, is that you? I need you to sign off on some paperwork."

"Sure, I'll be there in a minute."

The footsteps went by her office and on to Margaret's where the rustle of bags sounded suspiciously like someone returning from a shopping trip. Sherry cast an amused eye at Larry as they awaited her return. From Margaret's steps, they could determine that she had made a trip to the rest room and to the office break room, probably to get her tenth cup of coffee for the day, before she made her way back to Sherry's office where she opened the door.

"Sweet Jesus," Margaret screamed as she flung her entire cup of coffee against Sherry's office wall, "what is that thing?"

"This is Robby Robot," Sherry said in her most demure tone, trying not to burst out laughing at the dazed expression on her supervisor's face. "You know that referral you gave me about the kid at the Williams place? Well, here he is."

Robby cowered near Sherry's side and she put a supportive arm around him. Poor little fella, Sherry thought. Protectively, she said, "You're scaring him, Margaret. He's just a little thing."

"Scaring him?" Margaret yelled once more. "I nearly had a heart attack."

At that, Sherry and Larry couldn't keep their laughter from spilling out anymore, and Margaret blushed a vivid red with embarrassment. She was not the kind of woman who enjoyed being the butt of any joke.

"How do you know that thing is even safe to have in this office?" Margaret demanded. "Maybe he has a death ray or something and he'll decide to kill us."

"Robby hasn't done anything the least bit aggressive," Sherry said in her most defensive voice when she finally quit laughing. "I think he is more afraid of you than you are of him, Margaret."

Indeed, the little clicking noise had returned once more,

and Sherry could feel Robby's little gears clanking and knocking together in terror. She patted him several times in an attempt to soothe him while Margaret gathered her scattered wits.

"There is no way in hell we're going to find a foster home for that...that thing," Margaret pointed out. "What do you think you're going to do with it?"

"Robby was out there alone," Sherry reminded her, "and we didn't see a sign of anything else out there. Maybe he's lost or there's someone looking for him."

"'Lost'?" Margaret made an unpleasant face. "From where? A space ship? Is he an E.T.? Or do we need to call the mother ship?"

Sherry shrugged, her energy beginning to wane after the long day. "I don't know, Margaret. That's your decision. You said to find him and I found him. Now he's your business."

"Oh hell no," the older woman insisted. "You're not going to put that thing off on me."

"But you said you didn't want us working overtime, Margaret, and I've been working since..." Sherry checked her watch quickly. "Since five a.m. That looks to me to be ten hours just today. You said to keep it under forty. I'm pushing forty."

"Well, I authorize overtime then," Margaret snapped. "Take care of this and don't leave until you do."

"All right, I will," Sherry conceded without much fight. "Would you fax the placement form over to the regional office to see what they can find for me? I don't want to be here all night."

"Then you'd better take whatever they can find." Margaret stopped as she was leaving the office in her coffee-spattered suit. "Sometimes I think you go out of your way to see if you can gig me, Sherry, and this is about the worst thing you've ever done."

Margaret's admission was almost worth the price of the trip and the hours Sherry had spent walking through weeds, rubbish, chiggers, and mosquitoes, but it still didn't answer the question of what to do with Robby. If this had been one of the science fiction movies she liked, Sherry supposed that this would be about the point where the mother ship would float serenely to Earth and take Robby away. She waited a beat, then six or seven more, and nothing happened. So much for the movies, she thought. Of course, as far as reality went, Sherry had always figured that the least likely thing in the world to happen would be what they showed in the movies.

Larry finally broke the silence. "So, Sherry, are we going to sit around here all afternoon?"

"Whatcha mean, Larry?"

"Overtime, Sherry. I'm always glad to help, but you know I gotta justify my time and if we're just sitting here the boss isn't happy."

"Yes, I guess you're right about that. Let me see whether that placement fax has been sent back." Sherry looked around the corner carefully for rampaging parent robots. There was no one in sight except for Mary Lou who sat placidly at her desk filling out her time sheet.

Then the scene faded out.

For a moment Sherry saw nothing. Then a blast of heat and humidity hit her. For a moment, she thought that she had been here before.

The young woman looked around her frowning slightly. She had heard and seen no one, but there appeared to be signs of life around the old abandoned house. The cicadas, excited by her pounding, began to grind out their peculiar pee-ahh-pee-ahh, blanking out any other sound she might have heard, and Sherry Hayes put a long hand on an ample hip.

Then she turned from her position on the porch and she saw it. Was it an alien ship? It was definitely something she had never seen, something hostile in appearance and totally unearthly. She opened her mouth and tried to scream.

The sequence had ended unsuccessfully once more. This was a disaster.

"Our efforts remain futile. She resists the conditioning," Pnntt, the elder being, noted as they attempted once more to change the Earth creature's memories. It would never serve for her to report what she had seen and heard on this remote farm, but their need for privacy was inhibited by their great respect for all life. They did not want to destroy this being to protect themselves, but the secrecy of this mission was vital. She must not be allowed to tell any other human being what she had come upon.

"Yes," the other being agreed, "her mind is strong, particularly where the needs of the young and vulnerable are concerned."

"It is most unfortunate that she happened upon our craft."

"Yes, it is. Had she not been traveling in such a remote location, she might never have seen us at all." Ppssnn rubbed his knob anxiously. "Our records indicated that these beings rarely traveled in this location. These conveyances are also unlike the animal-drawn ones of the previous survey party. When we return, this must be corrected."

"Perhaps our information was in error."

"That much is certain. However, it cannot be helped now. We must change her memories or destroy her. I, for one, have never harmed another sentient being."

"Agreed. Let us try the conditioning again. Perhaps, this time it will work." Ppssnn manipulated the dials and knobs that would begin the sequence yet again, hoping for the sake of this creature that this time they would successfully change her memory.

TRAVELERS

By Kate Welty

Roger didn't know Lena well. It had been Maddie's raving one evening about how Lena always knew the latest trend, and how to push it, that made him consider approaching her.

"Oh Lena is brilliant! Just brilliant," Maddie enthused. It was so nice that Roger was taking an interest in one of her friends. Usually he seemed a little bored by her commentary on where she went, who she talked to, or what the latest shout-out was.

"Lena always knows what everyone is talking about and what they care about," Maddie told Roger. "And more than that! She somehow knows what they're going to care about next week, or next month. It's phenomenal. She's probably made and sold a dozen fortunes in the last few years, just by seeing what's going to be important and buying what's sellable ahead of the rest. She knows when people are losing interest too – or when they will."

"I don't know how she does it," Maddie added as she cuddled against Roger in their geltub. The gel flowed gently out of her way, its comforting warmth, cleansers and moisturizers invigorating her skin, but no more so than the gentle touch of Roger's hand smoothing down her back.

They were luxuriating in the pleasure of being together for a whole day instead of just a few hours. These last several months Roger had been home much less frequently. Most of the time his job had fairly regular hours, and they could plan to be together every evening and weekend. But ever since that night when he'd come home and wrapped her in a hard hug right at the front door, he'd been going to more and more meetings that took him out of Godmanchester for days at a time. Maddie hadn't paid much attention to the conferences Roger attended, because so often his work was confidential and he couldn't share what he was doing. But she could tell it had been a particularly stressful meeting this time, by how eager he was to shed his clothing and join her.

She smiled at him, struck all over again by how lucky she was to have this sexy, reserved scientist for her very own. Sometimes she worried that it was only her face and body he craved, since they were so different. She knew her face and features were nearly perfect. Her brilliant blue eyes, gold-blond hair and freckle-less complexion could have landed her a lucrative modeling job if she'd been a little taller and a bit more flat-chested.

Maddie knew Roger was smarter than she was. What if he got bored with her when her body got old and ugly? She thrust the thought away. Just the other day he'd said that anti-geriatric drugs and protocols were very nearly perfected. He'd frowned as he said it and added that it would just make Earth's problems worse. More people living longer lives would make it harder to feed the world's population and just add to the existing conflicts for land and water use. She didn't really understand it very well, but knew it had something to do with needing more land and water for food production, and conflicts between Eartholds and trashlands.

Maddie tucked the idea away to ask Lena about later. Maybe she wouldn't have to get old. Roger was the best thing that had ever happened to her. She couldn't lose him. Once she thought a child might keep him with her, but when she suggested they apply for a conception permit, he'd looked at her in dismay.

"I couldn't, Maddie," Roger had said, his face distressed. "I'm sorry, but the world that's coming-" He broke off and looked grimly into the distance and then said softly, "I can't tell you everything that I know; you must just trust me, but unless we can devise some solution we haven't hit on yet, I wouldn't want any child of ours to live in the world to come."

After the tub conversation with Maddie, Roger thoroughly researched Lena. He discovered somewhat to his surprise that Lena Cargill was just as much an expert in her chosen field as he was in his. Several successful businesses were registered under her legal name, Marlena M. Cargill, and all were closely related service companies; market research, event planning and promotion, and sales consulting. And just as Maddie's comments had suggested, all three companies had healthy bankrolls, showing increasing profits every year of the last five.

With due diligence satisfied, Roger decided Lena might be the very person to help the Society of New Nationalities ('SNN') introduce the Travelers to Earth society. If the public welcomed the aliens, SNN could begin to work through the difficulties of establishing a favorable trade agreement.

He did find it a little worrying that he'd found so little personal information on Lena Cargill. Perhaps, he thought, as a pop culture aficionado she knew how easily personal details could be ferreted out from blogs, websites, delivery services and purchase sites. Maybe she considered it good business practice to keep personal information off the net. It shouldn't matter except that it left Roger with no way to know what, beyond money, might motivate Lena to use her talents on SNN's behalf.

Roger was beginning to wish he'd asked Lena Cargill to meet with him somewhere else and not simply stop in here at his home. Granted the manor had the advantages of being comfortable and welcoming, yet still imposing with its centuries-old history, but he couldn't help but feel that Lena just wasn't taking him seriously. He wondered if a more business-like location would have been a better choice.

As Roger described the Travelers to her, and how a trade agreement with them would provide uncounted advantages to

Earth and all of Earth's people, she barely bothered to meet his eyes, and instead let her gaze roam the room. This week her hair was honey-brown, streaked with several different colors; green, yellow and blue, and curled riotously so that it looked almost as if a small flock of parakeets had decided to nest in her hair. He wasn't always home when Lena dropped Maddie off at the manor after the women's weekly outing, but he'd learned over time that the only thing about Lena that remained the same was her figure, and to a lesser extent her face. He couldn't say he was a fan of this week's look, but after almost two years with Maddie, he knew Lena would appear completely different by the next time he saw her.

She had a lush body, but her long torso and legs meant she carried the extra weight well. She could and did wear a miniskirt as effectively as tailored slacks or full length dress.

Today she was in a pantsuit that clung to every curve, with turquoise top, and rust pants, a long-sleeved hip-length maroon tunic and a canary yellow silk neckscarf. Her shoes were turquoise stilettos that exactly matched the top, as did her eye contacts. She had a horsey face; long and narrow with an almost roman nose. Her eyes were set well apart, and if her lips weren't as lush as her body, they at least weren't narrow. She varied her 'war paint' along with her clothing and hair. Her face might have seemed homely on a woman with a lesser personality, but the keen intelligence in Lena's eyes, her active nature and her habit of forthright speech made her attractive.

Roger frowned at her apparent disinterest, and started talking about the elegance of the Traveler ships, how everything they made and used was beautiful, just as they were. How valuable their knowledge could be, especially if there were suitable planets for Earth colonization within reach if we just had their method of interstellar travel.

Lena had pretty well tuned Roger out by then though, because after all, from her experience ships just weren't elegant. They were noisy and dirty and crowded full of people impatient to get from one place to another, and not real thrilled to be doing it with other people that they don't know, and don't want to know.

Roger almost sighed as his mention of interstellar travel was ignored. He was getting nowhere. Perhaps if he'd brought photos. Lena might respond better to the visual appeal of the Travelers.

Lena realized later that if she'd been paying more attention, she might have realized that there was something a little odd about Roger dropping the subject. He just didn't drop things. Once he'd made up his mind to let you in on something he'd secreted away in that rat warren of a brain of his, Roger would keep at you until he got what he wanted.

It was kind of funny considering he really wasn't much of a talker. He was more of a watcher, and a reader. Oh my, did he read. One night when Lena had dropped Maddie off a bit later than usual, back at Roger's ancient family home in Godmanchester, they'd found him ensconced in the library with four different books open at once. Roger had one open and upside down on each knee, one held upright somehow between the first and last fingers of his left hand (but he wasn't looking at that one) and another pressed open against the arm of the couch, with the index finger of his right hand tapping a line of text thoughtfully.

'Weird, that's all', Lena thought. 'Roger is just plain odd.'

She'd asked Maddie if he did that a lot, and she'd replied he did that multi-book thing whenever it was quiet enough. That he said it was only productive when the house was quiet.

'Productive,' Lena mused. 'That's what he calls it? Who talks like that?'

She reminded herself he was considered some kind of a genius among the people he worked with. One news blog had referred to him as 'the highly respected earthsystems bioengineering expert consultant Dr. Roger Kirkland' and there'd been a long string of letters after that. Hard saying what he actually did, but apparently it was important.

'So,' Lena thought, 'Maybe everyone talks like that where he works. They're probably like him. Maybe they even understand him.'

It did occur to Lena to wonder why Roger was so intent on telling her about the Travelers. After all, who was she? No one important; she wasn't political, had no HighHundred connections. She just had a knack for predicting buying trends. What he'd already told her was obviously more than what the general public knew. By now though, she suspected a lot of people were learning quite a bit more of the story. The media had been leaking stuff like crazy. Just yesterday morning she'd caught a part of a Blastoff! report during her commute.

The local news had suggested secret meetings were being held between SNN officials and aliens. The screen had displayed a photo of a deep sea research vessel. To Lena, it just sounded like an attempt to create airtime on a slow day. Especially since they admitted there'd been no confirmation or denial by any of the scientists supposedly in attendance.

But when the news had switched to a citizen report Lena had glanced up to take it in. Citizen reports were a lot less finessed than official news, and sometimes held grains of truth. She had listened with amusement to the dramatic intro:

> 'Blastoff! citizen reporter caught two scientists talking on Curieuse Island. Listen in now!'
>
> "That's right citizens, catch this crazy! Astrophysicists were heard arguing that the aliens, who they call the Travelers, must have observed some space phenomenon that Earth physicists haven't measured yet. That their technology alone couldn't make interstellar travel possible. Hear for yourselves!"

A vid had opened showing a woman and

man leaning over their lunches at an outdoor café. The woman was shaking her head vehemently. An insect flew into camera view and landed on the flowers centered on the table.

"I agree it ought to be impossible, but obviously it's not. They're here after all."

"So what does that mean? There is no way technology alone will make it possible to travel across interstellar space in hours instead of centuries, as they claim. Not unless our physics is wrong. And how could it be? It's based on consistent observable phenomenon. We couldn't have interpreted everything that incorrectly."

"Maybe we've gotten everything right that we've measured, but the Travelers' planet of origin was where they could see and measure some phenomenon that we're not in position to view. I don't get the impression that they're all that much smarter than we are, do you?"

"I guess not. To be honest, I find it hard to concentrate on what they're saying. I keep trying to get a better look at those wings-"

The woman had laughed and nodded, and the man reached an arm out for his glass and then waved the insect off of the blooms.

The reporter's face had swum into view again as she said quickly, "That's it, boosters! Too bad our mike in the sky got shoed off, but you heard it first from Blastoff! The Travelers are here – and they have wings!"

Lena had wondered cynically if the reporter had been tipped off to go to Curieuse or if she'd actually found the location all on her own. Lena suspected SNN administration liked it when all the scary ideas got dripped and leaked out bit by incremental bit. Then SNN could use public reaction to figure out where most people's opinions lay and shape the official story to fit right smack dab in the center of majority opinion. That way they wouldn't need to hire media relations staff to try to move public opinion to SNN's side.

Roger worked a bit like that too, Lena mused. He knew what he wanted. He knew he was a bit of an oddball from most people's point of view. And he knew that to get what he wanted, he'd have to figure out how to get other people's support.

'Maybe that's why he's so intent on telling me about it. To get a typical opinion,' thought Lena. 'Cause let's face it, I'm just about as normal as you can get. I'm always interested in the popular, especially what's new right now. I always know what's hot, and would never promote anything that isn't wiki'd this hour.'

Of course that took a lot of work because timing was everything. She had to pay lots of attention to all the new blogs because the ones without big followings yet, were the ones where something unique usually got started. But she still had to keep a fuzzycrawlir going in all the old ones, looking at all the current tags people used for something truly amazing, so she could tell when tags started changing. Then she had to feed all that into one of the predictive models. And since there were new and better tellmes released all the time, to keep her edge she was always looking for a new tellme too. But it was worth it.

Having her assistbot wake her at sunrise-minus 2 hours to point her to a new designer who departed a private jet in Paris just eighteen hours after her minor show in Brisbane? Ah, that was what it was all about. Getting a pre-order in for the first-off's before anyone else? Getting her pic flashed on the building-high displays in UpperNewYork because she sold her last sneakbuy at a ten-times profit? Not to mention scoring the highest number of kudos at the HighHundred Invitational Promenade.

'Oh, yeah,' Lena thought, 'That's what life is for; to

luxuriate in that thrill, in that moment of being right, of having figured it out first.'

So yes, maybe Roger knew what he was doing in tapping her. He must know she had her finger on the pulse of normal and he didn't. And even better, she understood motivations. Normal people wanted to be liked. They wanted lots of people to like them. Hell, they wanted to be loved. And it was easy to be liked, to be loved by lots of people, to be popular, if you just knew what was important right now. Today. Yesterday was so... over. Nobody cared about yesterday. But if you knew what was important today, and you talked that, walked that, wiggled your shoulders and stepped in that? Ah, then you would be loved... by billions.

The next time Lena stopped by after an outing with Maddie, Roger brought the Travelers up again, but this time he came at it from a different angle. He showed Lena photos of some of them, and of their ships. It took Lena only a few minutes to realize he was still trying to interest her in how to introduce the Travelers to the public and get public support for trading the aliens the 'products' they wanted.

Lena marveled at the range of patterns on their bodies, and squinted at the brilliance of their wings, and thought to herself that Travelers was a pretty boring name for a really flashy group of aliens. Or people.

Lena really couldn't quite decide if she thought they were people or not. Since she didn't know any of them personally, it was hard to judge. 'Perhaps', she thought, smirking a little, 'if I did know one of them I'd decide they were less alien than Roger.'

Roger sat there on the couch opposite her and tried with deadly earnestness to engage her in conversation. His gray eyes and extravagant sable lashes were exaggerated by the lenses of his old-fashioned rim glasses. Those eyes made her almost understand why Maddie found him attractive. It looked like he had a decent body under those five-year-old suits, maybe even a runner's build. If he would just lose the glasses, get a few new tailored suits, gray, and Italian, she decided, and then buy a personality, he wouldn't be half bad. Those smoky eyes were kind of hot, but the man was just boring as hell. He could grow that mink-brown hair a bit too, she thought. If he didn't always have it cropped to a bare inch or two it might actually wave a bit then and make him look less severe.

He had a nice enough face, but almost too smooth and expressionless. Lena tried to mitigate her boredom by imagining him with a goatee, a handlebar mustache, or just a nice dark shadow of stubble. Stubble, she decided, and maybe lengthier sideburns.

She was still deciding on the shape of the sideburns when Roger leaned forward and she reluctantly returned her attention to what he was saying.

"We need them, Ms. Cargill," Roger said, trying hard to capture her attention, "And they're an appealing people; smart, creative. Their ambassador is a lot like you. She's interested in knowing what people want, and she enjoys finding ways we might help each other. They think we are wasteful of-" and Roger paused as if he was deciding which word to choose. Finally he continued deliberately, "-our dead, and most of what we send to the trashlands. They would like us to trade all of that to them – for the science that will let us travel between the stars."

Lena Cargill laughed. Roger had to be joking. Of course he was.

'Give us your dead,' she thought. How teenage shriek-flik could you get? Even supposing he was serious, surely he didn't think anyone would sell Great Grandma to the alien bugs from outer space?

Roger knew he'd taken a chance telling Lena as much as he had. The news releases needed to be managed carefully, and so far leaks had been limited to a simple acknowledgement that SNN was in discussions with aliens. Roger still hoped to intrigue Lena enough in the Travelers that she might be willing to promote them. His research on Lena, and Maddie's description of what she was interested in, both suggested she was interested by new events and popular culture.

Roger eyed Lena musingly. He wasn't a very patient person, but he was persistent, and usually that meant he didn't really have to be patient for too long.

His fathers liked to tease that his Eartholder name would have been River. When he and his cousin were young, and argued about whether they would go fishing, or hike up into the foothills, or help collect insects, or anything else they thought of to do during Roger's summer vacations at the Earthold, Roger always got to do what he wanted, and his cousin Shale always gave in. "That's because," his father Tate said, with his mouth serious but his eyes smiling, "Even stone can be eroded by water, if water is persistent enough." But then his father Jerome grinned and countered, "Even water needs a bit of help. Roger must have a bit of grit in him too; kind of like you."

But so far, Roger realized his persistence in talking to Lena about the Travelers wasn't going anywhere. He needed help from Lena, or someone like her.

Earth had to have interstellar travel. No matter that the growth of scientific and engineering knowledge had been on a geometric curve since the start of the twenty-first century. Population growth was still on that same curve too, and so were food demands, trashland expansion, pollutant accumulation, and all the other measures of an overburdened world.

It had gotten to the point that there were virtually no undeveloped lands or shallow ocean surfaces remaining outside of the Eartholds. The Eartholds themselves had thankfully been expanded around the time that Roger had been born, and their protections strengthened. So the world did at least still have large pockets of biodiversity to help protect against the many threats that could decimate a single food resource. Food production was more diverse again, but

Earth's resources were still being taxed beyond its ultimate capacity to provide for its inhabitants.

Short of an enforced worldwide ban on conception, SNN needed new lands and oceans to colonize, and new places or ways to handle their trash and pollution problems.

The moon colonies had proven to be a drain on Earth's resources, and not as some had hoped, a realistic opportunity for expansion. Yes, they could keep people alive and productive there, but the energy that had to be expanded to build the infrastructure for terraforming, water and waste processing was still greater than the value of the products they were producing so far. It was not that Crater City or BellaLuna couldn't eventually attain economic independence, but that was likely still several centuries away, and Earth just didn't have that much time.

"Ms. Cargill, we will pay you well to simply provide your expertise – to introduce the Travelers to the public, and help present their interests to establish them in a positive light," Roger said, trying to be as direct as possible.

Lena tilted her head and looked at him in amusement, "Look, I can't handle that Ms. Cargill crap. I was Lena when I was just Maddie's friend, and you didn't want to talk me into something. Just call me Lena, all right?"

"What will persuade you, Lena?" Roger asked bluntly.

"Nothing," Lena replied, "Money isn't that important, okay? People make that mistake all the time, thinking money is what people want. Just think about it for a minute. What would it do to my rep if I backed some project people just don't care about? I'm not about to lose my pull over a bunch of alien insects that dropped in to give us a look-see. They've probably got a three-month window of interest, tops. Now, if more people cared, I might find a way to pop it, and my rep would still be good, but so far, they're just not top-thought."

Roger Kirkland clenched his jaw. She had a point, but if she truly understood, and cared about the future of... but she didn't, he realized. And neither did most other people in the world. Like Lena, they felt they had no voice and no impact on what happened on a global scale. How could one person out of billions make a difference? And how could billions be persuaded to act in concert? For the most part, the people of Earth lived in the moment, in only this moment, and pushed away uncomfortable thoughts of an uncertain and unlivable future.

Roger refused to give up. Somehow he had to reach her. "Lena," he tried again, "First of all, they aren't insects. Second – everyone has a dream. Some vision, some goal that is important to them, something that they think is impossible, unachievable. I promise you, if you will help us create a trade agreement with the Travelers that the public will support, you can ask for anything. Any impossible dream. And I promise you, that with the support behind me, I can make almost anything possible. You can have whatever you want."

Lena smiled and shook her head at him. "Not me, Roger. I don't have any impossible dreams. Sorry." And with that, she picked up her coat, gave Maddie a quick hug and headed home.

Lena set aside her inevitable thoughts on Roger's proposal. If she were perfectly honest with herself, she'd have to admit to a lot of curiosity about the aliens, and a tiny wish that she actually could play a role in sending ships out from Earth to colonize other worlds. It was a lovely romantic dream, but she was practical. She had to be. She didn't belong to one of the HighHundred families. Her future depended on how well she leveraged her abilities. She couldn't afford to take on a project she wasn't certain would enhance her reputation. She always weighed opportunity and risk, before making a wise choice.

She had only one weakness, and she hid it carefully. It was perhaps an obsession, but she preferred to think of it as a legacy. After all, it was her mother, a fan from earliest days, who first introduced her to the lore of the imaginary universe that was Galactic Heroes. Lena stepped into her living room, and then into the hall and opened the door to her Tribute Room.

It was little more than a large closet, and seemed even smaller since every wall surface was covered with images. Mounted center stage was the largest screen she could fit in the room – only 6x7, but the images there changed every few seconds. She smiled as just now it displayed the trailer for the worldwide release of the flic 'Galactic Heroes – Redemption'. Only sixteen more days and the exclusive, by invitation only, premier pre-release would play to a small audience of one thousand, nine hundred and sixty-six guests. The number of seats was rumored to be significant to true fans. Lena had secured an invitation through highly illegal, immoral and expensive means. She sighed again and shuddered with excitement. Only sixteen more days!

She let her gaze travel lovingly across all the images on the other walls. There was the manip her friend Tricia had made to her custom request, where her two favorite characters had their hands entwined while exchanging a kiss. Their eyes were closed and stars and nebulas filled the sky behind them. Their ship was there in the corner, not much bigger than the stars around it; but it was a small and recognizable symbol of adventure, commitment and courage.

With pleasurable anticipation, Lena settled into her livingchair, set the controls to cuddle and then signed in to her favorite fandom site. She had a couple of hours. Just enough time to enjoy the latest vid by her favorite artist.

"Look! Look, they're like butterflies! Wings! Look, Mom, oh, look! Wings! I want wings. Can I get wings?"

Roger stood to the side and watched as the very small, very select crowd of press agents, dignitaries, researchers, and a few tourists, got their first look at the Travelers. He would have preferred to have Lena's expertise to set up this event, and her help to evaluate reactions as well, but there'd been no break in her apparent disinterest.

"Oh, wow. They're like fairies! Look at them! Oh, they're all the colors of the rainbow."

"They're appearance is a help, at least," commented the policy expert standing next to Roger, as the tourists gushed at the handful of Travelers. The aliens were obligingly spreading their wings for display and walking in a little promenade behind the waist-high barriers that were designed to keep any overeager members of the public from getting too close.

"Yes," Roger agreed, "But the public doesn't know their place within ecological systems. Once that gets out, appreciation could turn to disgust. And when we tell people what SNN wants them to offer up for trade, so we can get that technology..." Roger frowned. He might not understand individual motivations all that well, but he'd been around enough touchy issues to know that the real trouble started when the public felt they'd been lied to, or tricked. Soon, very soon, they'd have to reveal more about the Travelers and what they wanted. He was likely going to have to cut his losses on the time spent trying to recruit Lena, and select some other promoter.

Roger kept worrying that some other group might get wind of the Travelers' interest in human remains, and decide to start a little private war. SNN hadn't dealt with anything more violent than a handful of demonstrations for over half a century. When all the real estate is already controlled by one consolidated government, the 'wars' over resources are fought in the boardroom of the invested businesses, and not on the ground.

War used to be profitable when whatever 'country' won got to control the real estate, the raw materials, and the workers. That all went away when destruction instead meant reduced profits for the consolidated invested businesses.

But it would only take a few mercenaries, stirring up enough dissent to create casualties, and war could become profitable again. Once investors realized corpses could be sold to the Travelers, how long would it be before businesses started weighing profit and loss between a reduction in the total number of customers versus a smaller number of better paying customers? Was there ever a war where the majority of soldiers had wealth on their side?

Roger might like to think that the Travelers would behave more ethically than the typical human corporation. But if decaying flesh was their favorite and most readily assimilated food, would they turn down human remains just because they were casualties of war? Could they even understand that a group of mercenaries, negotiating with them for starship technology independently of SNN, might not have the interests of all humans in mind? And if they understood, would Travelers care? No, he couldn't delay much longer. He would try to persuade Lena one last time, and if she still did not agree, he'd just have to hire someone else.

"Lena? Hey, Lena – pick up, will you? Where are you, girl?" Maddie said and then shrugged and pinched the implant in her earlobe to toggle her phone off. "I'm sorry, Roger. She's just not answering. I think she had something special planned for today. This whole last week she's been really distracted and hyped up."

Lena slammed through her front door, flung her bag to the floor and stalked to her Tribute Room. Once inside, she let her gaze move across the walls and her lip trembled until she bit down on it. Breathing heavily she stared at her vid screen. Every couple of seconds it flipped to a new promotion for Galactic Heroes – Redemption, or threw up a starburst vid of upcoming interviews with the GH stars. Lena leaned just enough to the right to reach her arm out to grasp a heavy promo item that she'd gotten at a GH con years ago and lift it off the shelf. She clenched it tight in her fist; her knuckles going white.

Her chest heaved as the news she'd been expecting went

live on the screen. Yells, excited chatter and demanding questions surrounded the director-producer of GH-Redemption as he turned a smug gaze on his audience and said, "Oh, yes, we were pretty sure there'd be a strong reaction to the pre-release. After all, Galactic Heroes has a strong fan base, and many of them have been waiting a long time for someone to bring new life to an old story. We're very pleased at the response."

"And you aren't afraid that you may have alienated some old fans by changing the essential relationship between the two character leads?" came a question from off camera.

"There's still plenty for the old fans to appreciate. There's lots of really edgy action, and we left all the old antagonists in place. But this vid was designed to attract new fans; fans that are looking for something different, for a new pairing to root for."

Lena's face went red with rage. All the pent up fury, betrayal and hurt she'd felt but had to suppress at the pre-release viewing surged through her now unrestrained. She screamed, "Bastaaaard!" at the screen, and hurled the heavy prop at the now-hated face of the director. The prop bounced ineffectively off onto the floor, and Lena flung herself into her livingchair. Unable to bear her sorrow and disillusionment another moment, she curled her body in on itself, and let the sobs take her.

"Lena? Lena?" A worried voice was coming from outside her Tribute Room. For just a moment, the old fear that someone might discover her obsession stabbed through Lena, but then a heavy coldness replaced that pang of dread. It didn't matter anymore. Galactic Heroes was dead. The bastard had killed it with his cheap introduced romance that split apart her two Galactic Heroes and destroyed forever their perfect pairing. All her dreaming, her fantasies, and her romantic notions about her two brave heroes facing an uncertain universe together, were dead.

"Lena? Lena, honey? Where are you? You're scaring

me," came Maddie's voice.

Stoically, Lena extricated herself from her livingchair, forced herself upright and opened the Tribute Room door. Maddie's wide eyes stared into hers from the middle of the outer room for a moment, and then her friend rushed forward and enveloped her in a hug. "Oh, sweetie. Whatever happened? You look awful!"

"I'm fine," Lena said hoarsely, "Just... just a little tired, that's all. What brings you over?"

"It was Roger," Maddie said. "He wanted to make sure you hadn't changed your mind before he hired someone else for his promo project. I told him if you said no once, you'd hardly-"

"Roger," Lena said slowly. "Roger. Is he here then?"

"He's just outside. I thought he'd better not come in. Just in case, well in case you had someone over or-"

Lena strode to the door and pulled it open. Roger drew himself up from where he'd been leaning against the wall and opened his mouth.

Lena forestalled him by demanding, "You said 'Any impossible dream.' Did you mean it?"

"Yes," Roger said.

The woman before him looked as if she'd recently suffered through some personal tragedy, but at his response she visibly straightened, her eyes glittered and she thrust her hand out at him like a weapon.

"You have a deal, Roger."

Lena strode confidently up to the Travelers' ambassador and offered her a handshake, a friendly smile and a speculative look.

"Hi. I think you're expecting me. I'm Marlena Cargill, but please call me Lena. I'm here to see if I can help with your trade agreement," Lena said briskly. The voder attached at the ambassador's neck made an almost inaudible series of low chirps. Up close, the ambassador didn't look at all like an insect. It was just that from a distance, the elongated fragile-looking wings, and the slender upright body looked similar in shape to some elegant wasp or perhaps a praying mantis. But standing near her, Lena could see that the ambassador's limbs and upper torso appeared almost furry. The individual hairs, if they were hairs, were much thicker than human hairs and densely covered the surface.

While waiting for the ambassador to arrive, Lena had looked around curiously at the other Travelers who were clustered in conversation with the human scientists. It seemed that there was almost as much variation in the color and shading of that fur as there was in the colors and patterns on their wings.

The ambassador briefly spread her wings and tilted them forward in Lena's direction and then folded them neatly back. They reminded Lena a bit of a stained glass window. Large sections of her wings were clear, but were bordered with jewel-colored patches of amethyst, ruby and sapphire. The entire wing had a kind of iridescence that reflected light back in a pearlescent shimmer. The ambassador's fur was mostly a pale sandy color, but in places shaded to light lavender. Her nostrils were situated on an odd-looking nose that seemed a cross between camel and dog. They flared slightly and then her front set of almost-human-looking eyes blinked. Except it wasn't exactly a blink; they irised closed and then opened again.

Lena frankly stared and then stuttered, "C-can you do that again?"

"Which?" asked the ambassador. Or rather, the question issued from her voder.

"Blink your eyes?"

The ambassador's nostrils flared again, and there was some minute change in the shape of the folds of skin under her nose before the ambassador very slowly closed her eyes. Almost like the mechanical lens on a camera, thin membranes of skin slid in spiral fashion from the outside edges of her eyes toward the center of her pupils until her eyes were completely covered, and then slowly they slid and spiraled back open again.

"Wow. That's cool," Lena said. "I don't think any Earth animals do that."

"No, we were surprised that there were no others on your planet with our arrangement of eyes. Some of your animals do have multiple sets as we do, but none are structured to open and close as our primary set does," said the ambassador. Her nostrils flared again briefly and she added, "I'm S'airai, by the way, and I'm very pleased to meet you."

Lena smiled back, and settled in for a nice long chat.

After S'airai left, having politely tilted her wings again as she departed, Roger sank down into the old-fashioned wooden chair at the conference table beside Lena and looked a question at her.

Lena looked back at him silently for a moment, and then said abruptly, "You need to leak some information about their basic biology. You've kept it under wraps too long. We don't want to set up any meetings with certain sectors of the public or industry until there's been at least a little speculation on how their biology might create an opportunity for them. We want them to be eager to meet with you; for a chance to build an advantage."

Roger nodded and replied, "Yes, I agree. There has just been a little concern about exactly what to write, what word choices would be least problematic, and whether it should be presented as a scientific paper, or as a news release-"

Lena laughed and said, "Oh citizen, you weren't kidding. You really do need me."

Roger looked puzzled and Lena shook her head in disbelief and added, "You read too much, and live too little. We're not going to do a news release and we're not writing a scientific paper either. We're going to have a dinner party."

As it turned out, the most difficult part of the whole event wasn't the security, or determining who would get an invitation, or even how much to charge. The most challenging part was the catering. Not a single human caterer Lena contacted was willing to even discuss a contract to provide the proposed Traveler menu that Lena (in strict confidence of course) presented. So in the end, Lena worked with S'airai to contract with a couple of the Traveler chefs. They would cater the meals for their people (in return for additional consumables) and Lena contracted separately, at ridiculous expense, for the menu items for the human attendees.

Lena did spend a significant amount of time carefully considering odor management, but simply holding the event in the open-air veranda off of a lovely Italian villa solved many difficulties. Arrangement of the banquet tables upwind of the serving centers, and situating backup fans across from them to blow any concentrated scent away from the seating area took care of most of the odor. She'd also arranged for the liquid refreshments to be served in the villa, just inside the doors off the veranda. That gave guests an easy excuse to depart into the climate and odor-controlled interior, ostensibly to refresh a drink. In addition, each guest packet for human attendees included a discrete nosefilter in chameleon flexfoam.

All in all, Lena thought, it was going well. She watched with interest as one reporter following intently along beside a Traveler and deeply engaged in conversation suddenly froze as their wandering took them downwind of the buffet of Travelers delicacies. Abruptly, the reporter made a short bow in the Traveler's direction and then made a beeline for the veranda doors. The Traveler looked after him in apparent confusion, but then just lifted her chin and followed her nose to the buffet to load up a plate.

Lena's lips quivered in amusement and she lifted her eyes to S'airai's. The ambassador's nostrils flared and she commented, "It was a brilliant idea to put all the liquid refreshments for your people indoors, Lena."

"Thanks, S'airai. It does seem to be working pretty well."

"Your people do seem to have considerable difficulty with the scent of our preferred foods. Is this why you so often bury or burn these foods; because you find the scent is unpleasant?"

"That might be a part of it, but I'd bet it has more to do with what we learned at our mother's knee."

"Mother's knee?"

"An expression for a learned behavior."

"Ah, I believe I understand. It is like a nymph insisting on a yellow cell wall because her tender preferred yellow."

"I'll take your word for it," Lena said. She hadn't quite figured out Traveler life cycles. Little things S'airai said suggested there might be more physical stages between birth, adolescence and adulthood than there were for humans, but the Travelers hadn't shared any images of their children yet. Lena found that protectiveness of their young rather reassuring.

S'airai's eyes squinted slightly and then reopened as she said, "I still don't understand the purpose of the banquet, Lena. It seems that you have gone to a lot of trouble and expense to entertain a very small number of people, and none of them represent the audiences you suggested will be most interested in contracting with us."

"Well, just because you were so gracious with my little catering problem, I'll let you in on a secret. The most important credential for getting an invite to this little party was to be a major blogger. These people don't necessarily represent anyone we'll want to meet with, but they do love to talk, and they love to stir the pot and get other people talking too, and they have huge followings. They're all really good at pushing the juicy."

S'airai tilted her head in inquiry and Lena explained, "That means talking about what is controversial."

"And we Travelers are controversial?"

"Not yet. But the lip-flapping has probably already started and in a few days we might just find that Traveler foods are controversial enough to get the whole world, and not just the scientific world, talking about you. When that happens, I'm betting that we'll have certain groups wondering just what you might be willing to offer them for all of their 'product'."

After the last of the attendees had gone, Roger and Lena sat together in the library of the villa as she brought up results from the fuzzycrawlers and tellmes she'd custom programmed. Roger sat tense and worried at first, frown lines forming deep in his forehead as extracts from the first blogs and their rampant emotionalism filled the screen.

'GROSS!!! Gagging!!! Just shows the boss upstairs has a sense of humor. Snort! WWJD? No idea, but what I did was RUN for an exit. The smell?! STAGGERING.'

'Oh my gosh, I don't know where to start. So, at first I thought they were really pretty, but then they started eating! And oh, you should have seen it. They have these long glistening tube things that look like snot that come out from these folds of skin or whatever under their noses and then they suck up the slimy puddles in their bowls. It was so creepy. I couldn't watch. Especially since, oh, it smelled awful. And those slurps! I've still got shudders!'

'Friends, do not, I repeat DO NOT accept an invitation to a Traveler's banquet. OMG I nearly lost my lunch. And the worst thing? If I had, it would have been their idea of a hostess gift. Whoda thought such pretty beings would have such disgusting habits?'

As Roger raised worried eyes to hers, Lena smiled faintly and shook her head at him. "Just wait," she said. "It'll be like this for hours, but then reader curiosity will kick in."

And sure enough, a few hours later the tellme results were sounding a little different.

'So, what do you mean, the smell was awful? Do you mean like anchovy bad, or old vomit bad?'

'Try NEW vomit bad. Really.'

'So, what were they eating? Did anyone say? Could you tell what it was?'

'Um, it's gross. Do you really want to know?'

'I asked didn't I?'

Roger was still frowning, but Lena, more experienced with how these things usually went, just sat back and waited patiently.

'You know, I realize it's pretty sick to think of, from a human perspective, but it's probably not unnatural for them.'

'What? Are you saying it's okay to eat stuff that is decaying? Rotting flesh, and partially digested crap? OMG, some of it literally crap?! NO!'

'Not for us, no… but for them…'

'Sick. It's just sick. I'm not talking about it any more!'

Roger looked across at Lena. She appeared bored, and had her vidspecs on and was twitching her fingers; playing some game that she'd told Roger she'd gotten from S'airai.

Suddenly she sat upright, pulled off her vidspecs and tapped at the screen. A little icon at the bottom bloomed to fill in the space and then lines of IM dialog started scrolling.

'J. J u bzy?'

'Sup?'

'U hurd bout those Flutterbys?'

'So?'

'What if we hd somethgn they wanted?'

'Not gittin u, bro.'

'They like gross stuff. 2 eat.'

'N?'

'Arnt u tired of pissin away r profit 4 trash pikup?'

'U got better idea?'

'Those Flutterbys. U thinkmayb theyd buy it off us?

'R trash?'

'Yeah. Why not?'

'What they gonna use 2 pay us with?'

'Maybe we could trade for somthn?

'Like what?'

'I duno. Somethin?'

'UR fulovit, Oz.'

"There!" Lena said. "That's what we were waiting for. Okay, now you can start a release or two. Nothing too obvious; 'Travelers and SNN officials in talks on possible trade agreements.' Something like that. A few days, maybe a week later, bump it up to 'SNN officials agree to facilitate meetings between Traveler representatives and representatives of publicly owned aglands and trashlands.' NOT privately owned. No dates, nothing specific. I'm guessing that will be enough to have those industry sectors, especially the for-profit ones, pushing hard for their inclusion in those meetings. SNN ought to be able to take it from there.

"Set your terms high. They can earn tax credits from SNN for making their 'raw materials' available to Travelers at a fixed SNN-negotiated price. Your trade agreement can just state that Travelers provide technology and technical assistance to SNN in return for SNN brokering sales of that commodity."

Roger stared at the screen and then back at Lena and asked, "You're sure?"

"Absolutely. If those two dumbasses have figured out an angle, then you can be sure the smart girls and boys in corporate trashland and agland industries have too; they're just keeping it all on the QT. That's a good sign; it means they think it's worth keeping quiet."

"What about the mortuary industry?"

"Don't do it."

"But the Travelers – they were pretty specific about how wasteful they thought that-"

"I don't mean we shouldn't trade them bodies, Roger. I mean we shouldn't let the mortuary industry get those contracts."

"Why? What do you suggest then?"

"You said one of our population problems is that people are living longer. We both know that's not the worst of it. Most seniors can't compete for a good wage anymore with the younger generations that are working, can they? So they're not only getting older and needing more care, but they've got less money to support themselves. Except for HighHundred types, most of them are moving in with kids or grandkids… and Roger, nobody's happy with that. I'm sure you could show me stats on reported elder-abuse, but I'd bet it is barely a blip on what's really happening."

"And?" Roger asked frowning, wishing he could dispute it.

"So let our elders sell the Travelers an interest in their bodies as a kind of reverse insurance policy. Here and now, they get a little extra per month income from their policy. When they pop off, the policy matures and Travelers collect the corpse. No mortuary expense; the family doesn't have to choose what to do with Grandpa since he didn't leave a will…"

Roger stared at her. "It would kill the mortuary business."

Lena chuckled. "Good one, Roger."

"I'm not kidding!"

"No, no, I know you're not. But really, don't you think it's a better idea?"

"Maybe, but I doubt SNN will want to broker it. The government is supposed to protect industries, not eliminate them. If SNN starts destroying one industry, the rest will start to wonder if they're next."

"SNN doesn't need to broker it. I don't see why the

Travelers can't operate their own business to buy that particular 'luxury item' independently from SNN."

"Where will they get the credits?" Roger asked.

"They're a smart people, I'm sure interstellar travel isn't the only product they have to offer," Lena responded.

"You're probably right," Roger conceded, glancing at the frozen image of the game on her handheld. It was oddly mesmerizing, and game-playing was a huge industry, a much larger one actually than the mortuary business.

"So, Roger," Lena said slowly when he seemed to be done asking questions.

"Yes?"

"I've held up my end of the bargain. When do we start work on my impossible dream?"

With Roger's assurance that he'd already set people to work to accomplish her 'dream', Lena gathered up her coat and her game, but then paused thoughtfully and sat back down to put in a call to S'airai. With Roger's tacit agreement to let elders make their own deals with the Travelers, she had a few suggestions for S'airai.

Lena gave Maddie a quick hug and unlocked the vehicle door so she could step out. As Maddie paused at the door to the manor and waved a cheerful goodbye, Lena's brow wrinkled. It had been a few weeks now since she'd last talked to Roger, and since she'd sent S'airai some ideas on how the Travelers might step things up a bit. No news was usually good news, but perhaps it was time to check and see that everything was going well. Lena pulled out her handheld and tapped the screen. Soon the new tellme she'd programmed popped up articles.

Travelers Ambassador Meets With UARP

The United Association of Retired People today announced that the presentation

160

'New Opportunities for Elder Income' has been added to the offerings at their annual convention to be held next week, and will be presented by Ambassador S'airai of the Travelers. A reception room will be available following the convention, so attendees may meet with the Ambassador to discuss this important and exciting new revenue stream for retirees.

The UARP understands that many of the more than two hundred and twenty million members will be attending the conference remotely, or have subscribed to receive transcripts, and assures members that even though this presentation is a late addition to the conference, it will still be included in remote feeds and transcripts.

Allied Senior Care Facilities Inc. Signs MOU With **Travelers**

President and CEO of ASCF Inc. announced yesterday that a Memorandum of Understanding has been signed between the company and Traveler representatives.

Under the MOU all new and future residents of ASCF Inc. worldwide, and their advocates, will be provided with information packets on how to enroll in the Travelers MyChoice program. Packets include detailed Traveler disposition policies and options to aid seniors and their advocates in making the choice that is right for them.

Allied Senior Care Facilities Inc. is proud to be the premier licensor of 'Best of Times' end of life options on the planet, serving more than thirty-seven million elders daily.

Lena let go a sigh. S'airai seemed to have things well in hand, and even if she ran into a problem, they could just get together over lunch, or, Lena amended hastily as she remembered some of S'airai's favorite foods, they could get together *after* lunch and talk things over. In fact, thought Lena, maybe she'd see if S'airai wanted to meet even if things were going well. The game S'airai gave her was addictive as hell, but it lacked a little personality. Lena couldn't help but wonder what a good designer might do with the game if he had the opportunity to integrate characters from fandom like Galactic Heroes. They'd need to obtain licensing rights, of course, but... Lena hummed thoughtfully to herself and set to work programming a new tellme.

It was time. Roger had finally sent word that her Impossible Dream was completed. Lena took a breath and then opened the door and stepped into her newly designed flat. She hadn't asked for a remodel as a part of her price; Roger had done that without her request. He'd purchased the next-door flat, had the wall between removed, and rebuilt her Tribute Room to triple its original size, while almost doubling her living space. He'd gotten contractors in to update the entire flat, and presented her with a 100-year pre-paid lease. She'd just stared at it, then stared at him, and then at that piece of paper in her hands.

Beside him, Maddie stood grinning.

"Your idea?" Lena asked Maddie.

"The basic idea, yes, but he kinda went crazy with it."

Lena looked at Roger and his expressionless face and realized suddenly that there was a shy little boy buried underneath. She shrugged first, and then moved forward and gave him a big and almost-fierce hug.

"Thanks," she mumbled.

One side of Roger's mouth hitched up, and then he shrugged too and said, "You are welcome."

"You two!" Maddie said in exasperation and then started to drag Roger out of the flat. "C'mon you softie. She's going to want to see her Impossible Dream for the first time all by herself."

So now Lena felt mossunderfoot floors. Smartglo lamps brightened as she started down the hall, and dimmed as she left them behind. There in her new Tribute Room were two completely programmable livingchairs AND a livingcouch. And best of all her new vidscreen again took up the largest wall, only now the wall was huge.

Lena took in a deep shuddering sigh of anticipation and then curled up on her livingcouch and said softly, "Let's go."

The screen in front of her glowed and then slowly a starscape filled in, with triumphant music building in volume and tempo. From a tiny pinpoint of light indistinguishable from one of the many distant stars, a golden ship grew larger and first swept elegantly past; slowly enough that the ship's name emblazoned along one shining flank could be contemplated. Then that lovely emblem of so many fan dreams curved away fast and then slowly circled back. As the ship re-approached head-on and the music reached its crescendo, words filled in below the screen: Galactic Heroes – Tribute.

Lena smiled with satisfaction as the screen filled with her beloved characters. It was perfect, just perfect.

The next day, Lena's smiles became grins as she reviewed

headlines.

Cloud Theft? Users Scurry to Check Their Accounts

Cloud Sites Deny Vulnerabilities Even While Investigating

Vidworld Reeling At Gone-Missing 'Galactic Heroes - Redemption'!

Lena's eyebrow went up and with a lower lip clenched between her teeth, she started reading the Vidworld news.

Fans, if you're one of those who paid your credit for the long-awaited release of Galactic Heroes – Redemption, and are wondering what happened to your virtual copy in the Cloud, you are not alone. Everywhere copies were stored, the vid seems to be missing. Even more mysteriously, copies that were listed for sale in any online venue, just hours ago, are now out of stock.

Trying to find a copy in a local hard-media store? Good luck! Our reporter used a calling tree to try to find just one copy and came up empty. Attempts to reach the producer or any actor associated with the vid for comment failed as well.

Now for the real kicker! Search anywhere, anywhere at all for the words 'Galactic Heroes – Redemption' or just 'Galactic Heroes' and you'll see a pop for a new vid, available now, of 'Galactic Heroes –

Tribute'.

We bought that baby and popped her in and guess what? Our boys are back together! Going just by memory of GH-R, 'cause we just told you we can't snag a copy, this new vid is virtually a redo. Except of course that the 'new relationship to root for' the director touted to the dismay and rage of many old die-hard fans is completely gone. Instead, the boys tackle a new villain! That 'new relationship' character is still there, even with a few new scenes and more character development than we recall from GH-R, but she's not a wrecking ball!

What's a fan to think? Here's what I think. This new GH-Tribute IS a tribute to Galactic Heroes! It's better than GH-R ever was. That was just a kick in the pants and an affront to the series. Let's let a bad dog lie, shall we?

Lena grinned gleefully at that last sentence, and reflected that the fan sites were probably at max capacity. She could hardly wait to sign in. Roger might be thrilled with a signed SNN / Travelers trade agreement, and the recently announced plans for joint exploration of habitable planets, and yes, Lena had to admit she felt some satisfaction at helping to make that possible. But really, when it came right down to it, she knew she was going to get more joy and excitement, just hearing how fans reacted to her Impossible Dream.

Edited by Sam Taylor

THE TROUBLE WITH COUGHING

By Patricia Burn

"Come and start a new life on Proxima Centauri Prime," they said. Remember that? No one said a thing about the lung worms, right? But hey, I'm getting ahead of myself. Where should I start explaining this to you? The beginning seems a good place. Where would that be? Let me think...

Well, as you might remember, around the beginning of the 23rd century, Earth was getting pretty crowded – population, twenty-one billion. Mars was fully colonised with seven billion under bio-domes, a revolution to secede from Earth's authority already ancient history, and a row of battle satellites enforcing the 'No More Earthers' rule. The Moon was pretty much reduced to a mined-out pile of rubble. Mankind's two populated planets weren't talking to each other and, all in all, things were looking pretty bleak and tense. It was time to look elsewhere for somewhere to live. Obviously, the place we decided to look first was the place that was nearest; the Alpha Centauri cluster. Quite some time back, long range observation had revealed there were several planets there that were worth a look, so why bother travelling anywhere further?

Typical Earth mentality, right? Even after we kicked up a head of steam behind the idea to go, the politicians and various corporations spent twenty years talking and bickering about what to do and how to do it. Then, having figured that out, they spent some twenty more pooling their resources and merging some countries into mega-States. Finally, they got around to building us some brand new interstellar laser drive star ships. Mars had no ships of any sort at this point you understand - bar several surface-jumpers - as Earth had seen fit to withdraw all its spacecraft in a fit of owner's pique when Mars seceded. And had then slapped on an export ban, topped up with the threat of total asset seizure for anyone - individual or corporation - found helping Mars to get their hands on a space-worthy craft of any kind. That way, you see, EarthGovt could charge the Martians majorly sky-high bloody export taxes for anything they wanted from them - and they did. It was no wonder the planets barely talked at a diplomatic level anymore 'round about back then.

When they noticed Mars was building its own laser ship there was a great big hoo-hah. Suddenly everyone was talking about the possibility of Mars colonising Alpha Centauri and beating Earth to it! Things were tense for a while. There was very nearly a war, my dad said, when the Mars ship launched. Boy, did everyone on Earth laugh when it headed towards Venus instead! The Martians were always more practical than Earthers. Let's face it, when you live under a dome one planet is much like the next. You might as well live on the planet that's nearest. I've a lot of time for Martians. Good people, most of them.

Where was I? Oh, right. Well, that crisis passed and several Earth Ships went out towards our nearest star. My dad was a young man living in Antarctica at the time. He didn't really take much notice of what was going on in the world or off it, to be honest: he had too much to do at home. This was all before I was born, you understand. I grew up surrounded by beautiful fields of arable farmland; 157,000 acres of high yield wheat which it was my father's job to manage and control. I loved living in one of the old-time nature reserves. Give me good old-fashioned food instead of manufactured proteins and nu-complex carb compounds any day of the week. Of course, there weren't many people on the planet in our position to be able to say that. The only reason natural foodstuffs were in production on Earth at the time was for the indulgence of the rich and to maintain the 'natural' humanly supportive biodiversity of the Earth for transplantation to another planet at some point so we could go there and start again and try not to ruin that one.

The first ships that went out were all research vessels. Three ships went out in the first wave: the Pegasus, the Ondine and the Meltemi. They could have sent one ship but they were playing safe - hedging their bets - because the Interstellar Laser Drive was new and deemed, at best, 'experimental' over the very long distances it'd need to go for this trip. I reckon they weren't actually sure that all of them were gonna be able to make it, if the truth be told, so sending three was the best way to make sure at least two got there and at least one came home again. Me, I'd have sent four, to be on the safe side.

Time was the main problem back then of course, as even at one-tenth the speed of light the journey was going to take more than forty years out and forty years back. Cryogenics was a farce; ice burns were a bitch and most people came out with the IQ of a cabbage, or stark staring mad. And bald; freezing did a number on hair follicles every time. Generation ships had been considered but then, who really wants to set out on a journey knowing they've got to procreate along the way, teach their offspring all they know, and die before they get home? Not me. Think about it, what if your kid didn't want to be a scientist or was just too plain dumb to do the math to get you home again? Not my idea of fun. A few people were up for it, of course, but the powers that be decided there had to be a better way.

The better way involved playing God. Doesn't it always? Pretty neat idea actually. Create a mini-universe in the cargo hold where time goes slower, move all but two of your crew into it for the duration of the journey, and bring them out again when you get to your destination. (It also means that you don't have to carry as much food and other provisions for the journey. Pretty practical really.) The elapsed time for the people in the bubble universe would be about five days. All they had to do was take a couple of sandwiches in there, a couple of flasks of tea, a few deckchairs, a pile of books to read, and before you know it, you're there. Of course the journey was a lot slower – forty-something years slower – for those left outside. The psych evaluations for the two left outside were more important than their piloting and engineering skills, to be honest. They did get to ride in the cargo hold on the way back though as it was figured the ship could make its way back on its own. After all, it had the Earth Beacon to latch onto and heading home is apparently a heck of a lot easier than setting out, for reasons to do with interstellar space travel that I know nothing about.

Interesting thing about the bubble universe; the scientists had been trying to perfect these for years in the labs - but hadn't been getting anywhere. In the end they bought in the technology from the private sector, where they found it existing by accident without anyone actually knowing what they really had. It seemed one of the minor players in the waste industry had covertly opened up what it thought was a wormhole to someplace – they cared not where – in an old empty mine in the Urals and had been pretending to be illegally burying waste in there, landfill style, whilst actually tipping it into the 'wormhole' and scattering it in space, or so they thought. They got rid of several billion tonnes of rubbish this way - rather than hauling it out in freighters to add to Saturn's rings, as they'd been contracted to do. Eventually, of course, someone had noticed container after container of domestic waste going down into the mine and coming up empty and had figured out that the size of the natural cavern they were supposedly ignoring being illegally filled up must be bigger than the moon and one thing led to another. Questions were asked. Answers were found. People were arrested for jeopardising the structural integrity of the planet. Scientists realised what they really had. Deals were made and pleas were bargained out. And a trip was planned to Alpha Centauri.

The fact that there was a bubble universe in existence that contained approximately 2.75 billion tonnes of Earth's domestic waste seemed to get overlooked somewhere along the way. Someone just cut the umbilical and sent it on its way. Best not to think about that bit too much.

Once they learned to calibrate space-time - how to set its 'speed' so to speak - within the bubble (by varying how they added energy and mass to the monopole - I mean everyone knows that now, like 'Albert says E equals MC squared' you know? But at the time it was News...) - once they figured that one out, they were away. Pretty quickly too. Within six months actually as, hell, solving the problem of how to keep people alive all the way there and all the way back again had been the only thing stopping us setting off in the first place. It only took as long as six months because they had to make sure the bubble universe was actually going to stay stable, keep everyone alive inside it, and let them step out again after five days/forty-something years/whatever completely unchanged. They got it right by bubble universe number seven and the friends and families of those who "went missing" in bubble universes one to six got a nice payoff.

EarthGovt prevaricated and blithered over a myriad of minor issues but one day there seemed to be nothing left to blather over and so finally, three nice new shiny interstellar laser drive star ships - "iLADS" they called them - each one manned and womanned by eight of Earth's best astronauts and scientists, set out for outer space on Wednesday, 14 July 2252 A.D.

If each ship got there in one piece and no one was lost along the way, eighteen of the astronauts would get to Alpha Centauri around about five days later. And for the other six it would take a little longer. Forty-two years longer to be more precise. But what's a little time between friends? Lord only knew what year it would be when they got back. If they got back. Everyone on Earth wished them luck. Most people on Mars and Venus really didn't give a fuck.

From our perspective, here on Earth, not an awful lot happened after the Big Launch; bit of an anticlimax really. Although, building interstellar laser drive star ships did become big business for a while. Fusion was so last century. Before long, the New World Government began to amass the beginnings of a fleet of iLADS. No one took much notice. We still weren't talking to Mars and now they'd colonised Venus we weren't talking to them either. Life went on as normal.

My dad remembers that whilst radio-communication was still possible there was "talk" between Earth and the three ships for a while but when it got to the point of waiting for months for a reply to your question there really didn't seem much interest in the media for continuing a dialogue.

I remember learning at school that the Light Bead bearing the information packet signalling that they were all still alive and that everything was perfectly A-O.K. on the ten year anniversary of the mission's launch - from their perspective - from their *pilots'* and *engineers'* perspectives - came in on Friday, 17 July 2263. I remember latching onto that with a grin and a feeling of significance - because that was the date on which I was born.

There were plenty of other dates to learn of course. 'Dates on which Earth-kind had Courageously Set Out For The Stars' per the schoolbooks. 'Dates on which EarthGovt chose to utilise obsolete iLADS so they could build some new ones' per the sceptics. But I guess it made sense. After all, why put all your eggs in one basket. Just because Alpha Centauri was closest there was no need to assume that we were going to find everything we needed there. EarthGovt had its interstellar scientists draw up and arrange a list of constellations and planets to check out in order of habitability potential shortly after the first ships set out. And fleets of three ships had gone out every three years or so, ever since.

Deep-Space travel was boring. A perpetual sink for resources and people, the cynics said. People left. No one ever came back. Nothing ever happened. Until it did.

~~It was my 40th birthday. My wife Maria, a~~

Hey, sorry about that, where was I? I was 'off-line' for a few Planck lengths there, just for a 'moment' - to use the old phrase. I guess the Proxies were giving me a bit of a polish. Can't have your Earther getting dusty now can we. Ah, the problems of corporeality. I sometimes forget I still have a "body". It's also pretty weird talking to you in "real time". Absolutely not used to talking to somebody in the body, here. We'll get you adapted soon enough. Don't worry. The coughing will soon stop.

Life here is pretty good you know. You will get used to it. Right yes, back to subject. Orientation. You still don't know what's going on, right? No collective memories yet - just the sense of self and that damned cough. Yea, I remember that. Must stop rambling and get back to subject. 'Don't know how you got here or what's going on.' My job to fill you in. Okay.

Welcome to Proxima Centuri Prime. In less than three hours you'll be unconscious. In three days' time you will be dead. Unless you listen very carefully to what I am about to say.

My name is John Grant. I was Captain of the Neddermeyer, the ship of scientific exploration sent here to confirm the positive finding of the Pegasus that this place was in fact fit for human habitation. I sent the affirmation. It's my fault you're here. Get over that. You are the 180 plucky 'volunteer' pioneer settler scientists who just happen to also be in perfect health, fully fertile and of suitable breeding age, chosen by EarthGovt to follow me out here to see if I was right about this place. Your ship, the Daedalus, will be both the first and the last of any fleet of colonising iLADS to land upon this godforsaken rock. Just as you, all of you, will be the last humans who will ever come here - as this planet is now subject to an intergalactic quarantine and is permanently off-limits to all mankind.

Damn, that was heavy wasn't it? Normal service will be resumed as soon as possible. Seriously folks, there are some things that you just have to spell out with your serious hat on. Even if you don't want to.

No. Stop it. For Gawd's Sake, people, do not start *doing* things. Just sit down, concentrate on breathing, and listen to what I have to say. Thank you. There is no point *doing* anything. There is nothing to be done. We tried *doing* everything ourselves, the first time around. And we had longer than you've got; we'd only just dug the soil at that point. You have no time at all. The soil is long since dug. The worm has long since multiplied and the air is long since poisoned. Sit down and listen if you want to live. You need to take this in and understand what is going on because I cannot save your lives without your permission.

I said, SIT DOWN. I do not want to have to *make* you sit down, but then again, if I have to, I will.

Yes, I *CAN* MAKE YOU SIT DOWN. All of you. At ONCE. I can do a lot of things. I am no longer entirely human. And nor will you be for much longer – unless you choose   to   die.
I said, SIT! Shut up! And listen. And concentrate.

Perhaps it would be better if I turned off your collective

sight centres and gathered you together in a virtual conference room of some sort?

(Turns on hologrammatical representation of former self and enters lecture mode.)

There. Is that better? Sit your virtual bodies down somewhere and watch inside your heads. Do I have your attention, *now?*

Thank you. I hope you have begun to understand the gravity of your situation.

(Increases perceived gravity by 10%)

I said "Shut up and listen." You're dying and you need to listen. Thank you. (About bloody time too.)

(Now, where was I, *again.*)

History. Right. Listen, take mental notes and take this in. You have some choices to make very soon and your future depends entirely upon you listening to what I'm about to say, you understanding what I have said, and you deciding what it is that you want to do about it.

Yes, I know you don't feel very well. Think about it; that underlines the fact that I'm telling you the truth, right? Listen to what I'm saying and concentrate. Listen only to my voice. Concentrate on me. You are the crew of the Daedalus.

- 79 strong and healthy men, aged between 22 and 53.
- 99 strong and healthy women aged between 20 and 36.
- And your dear sweet pilot and co-pilot, Mr and Mrs Rogers, current ages 72 and 74 respectively. Ain't love grand.

You landed here on Proxima Centauri Prime approximately 1 hour ago after a forty-something year voyage – which felt like five days for most of you – and you began to die the second the air locks were opened.

You have some decisions to make. Here is the history behind what you need to know.

Each of those first three ships made it to the Alpha Centauri cluster intact – more or less. There was a miracle in and of itself, but also a story for another time.

Being slightly closer than the main star system, obviously Proxima is always going to be the first to be checked out. They were pretty pleased to find that gas giant you see up there filling our skies right now, but when they found this ball of mud moon going 'round it... hehe... when they realised the gas giant was in the Goldilocks Zone – do you people realise how goddamn *narrow* the goldilocks zone of a red dwarf this goddamn small is? – and this gas giant was sitting there, right slap bang in the middle of it, with a mudball moon in a weird geo-stationary orbit above, it no less – well, they drew straws to see which of them was gonna get first dibs. Pegasus won – or so they thought – and the Meltemi and the Ondine headed out for Alpha Centauri A and B. Never did find out what became of them. I'm sure the Proxie know but they've never told me.

The Pegasus sat there at the edge of the system and mapped this place for a bit before coming in for a closer look. They had just enough time to send another light bead back to earth saying they'd found what pretty much looked exactly like a textbook 'planetary body worthy of further investigation' (PBWoF i) before a coronal mass ejection blasted them into oblivion whilst they were orbiting around the bright side of the gas giant. Oops. Do you think maybe there's a reason this planetoid's in permanent geostationary orbit slap bang mid-centre above the night side of its humongous brother up there? Ha! You betchya. Smart people, the Proxie. What, you don't think this moon is natural, do you? Think on.

Anyways, moving on. Light bead gets back to Earth. I'm forty-two when it gets there – deal with it; you are Doppler shift's bitch. Earth Govt is rapt by the news – "Hey, a potentially inhabitable mud ball! Let's send some people there!" – and pulls me, and nineteen other 'Earth Scientists' and 'Land Technicians' out of our current cosy projects where we're nicely settled in our happy little lives so far out of our comfort zones within a few weeks we're not even in the same solar system and puts us in an iLADS "all-you-can-eat" alternate reality bubble universe buffet for five days going on 42 years undertaking an intensive home study course in all you could possibly want to know about examining a mud ball in outer space for potential habitation by human beings, together with 6 flyboys and a squad of grunts and muscle for company.

Got to love Earth Govt, right?

Is any of this ringing any bells with any of you yet? Something very similar will have happened in each and every one of your lives when *my* message got back to Earth. That's how *you* ended up here.

I'm sorry about that. As I said before, my bad. I'll get you through this as best I can, okay? Try to stay calm. Breathe deep and regular. When the coughing starts, remember it *will* stop. When it does, spit.

Concentrate on this next bit, especially.

We got to Proxima Centuri – that's PC to you and me - in just over five days, our time. Our pilots, unlike yours, decided they wanted to take turns so rather than one pair of them taking the helm for the entire journey, all forty-two years of it, they divide it into six seven-year stints with them all doing two stints each, the desired outcome being they'd each only be fourteen years older when we got there. Of course, it was pretty weird seeing them come back in after a twenty hour shift looking seven years older each time. But I guess not as weird as seeing Mr and Mrs Rogers over there age forty-two years in five days was for you lot, eh? Ringing any bells yet?

Ahh, a spark of recognition. We start to get there. Good. You've got to remember who you were before you can decide who you want to be.

Sam and Dodo were the pilots for the last leg of our voyage. Which was damn fortunate really. Both of them are experts in stellar cartography and the planetary sciences. If we hadn't had them at the helm, to be honest, we might have gone the way of the Pegasus. Four weeks out from the PC system – pilot time – the two of them relayed a message through the time buffers for us to come out of the hold early. As 3.3 minutes in the BU is equal to a week in the cockpit it took us a couple of days to rendezvous with them but when we did we too were way beyond fascinated by what we saw. "Fuck me" seemed to be the general consensus once everyone had wrapped their brains around what the figures were showing us.

Pay attention to this bit because the chances are even if you remember anything whatsoever about the Alpha Centauri system, what you think you remember is wrong.

Alpha Centauri. Rigel Kent. Brightest star in the constellation of Centaurus. Third brightest star in the night sky. 1.34 parsecs from Earth. How many light years is that? You at the back, in the red shirt. 4.37 light-years? Quite right. Give the man a gold star! Thing is, Alpha Centauri isn't a star, it's a system. A binary star system. Two stars. Alpha Centauri A and Alpha Centauri B. Alpha Centauri A is a bit bigger than our Sun and one and a half times as bright. Alpha Centauri B is a bit smaller than our Sun and less than half as bright. A bit like some of you. Both of these whizz in an eighty year orbit around a common centre never more than the distance between our Sun and the former-planetary-body-known-as -Pluto, apart.

All of that is irrelevant. Because there is also a third star known as Proxima Centauri. Why the hell it's not called Alpha Centauri C is beyond me. Let's not go there. And that was the place we were heading to. That was the place from which the telemetry had been tweaking the antenna of Sam and Dodo for over a year before they brought us out of the BU to take a look at what they were seeing in real time. That's the place we now are. The first thing you need to wrap your head around is it's not here by accident. There is nothing 'natural' about Proxima C.

Get this, the entire Proxima system is basically floating around out here by choice. It's a pretty little thing. Emphasis on little. When we set out we thought it was gravitationally bound to Alpha Centauri A and B. It's not. It's merely lolloping along beside them in a vaguely hyperbolic trajectory.

Its current association with A and B is purely a celestial flyby, a place to park, and enjoy the scenery. Everything about this system is designed by the Proxie. One nice little Red Dwarf parked in a convenient wing of the galaxy. One great big gas giant to mop up any debris in the System. Said gas giant conveniently the right distance from the sun - in the Goldilocks zone as far as we're concerned. One three-quarter-Earth sized iron cored oxygen-nitrogen-atmosphered moon with salt water seas, icecaps at both poles, two sizable continents and several minor islands, subterranean fresh water flows and carbon-based vegetation, a regular home from home mudball in geostationary orbit and conveniently synchronised with the rotation of the gas giant around the red dwarf to the extent that every time the regular pattern of peak and flux of solar activity reached its apex the moon is conveniently situated around the far side of the planet, so the gas giant is always shielding it from the massive destructive stellar winds, magnetic storms and coronal mass ejections blasting from the surface of the star with a mathematical regularity matched only by the regularity of its own dance of synchronicity and cosmic placement. Nothing like a massive gas giant parked between you and your star every time it farts gamma rays, XRAY radiation, cosmic radiation heat radiation blah blah blah at you, eh boys? It all looked a little "designed" to Sam and D and, frankly, we agreed.

Now, if you're confronted with 'design' on this scale, you're either talking 'deity,' or 'seemingly omniscient alien life form,' right? Clue; this place didn't turn out to be the Garden of Eden. Or maybe it did, depending on your theology.

Don't forget to spit when you cough. You'll stay conscious longer that way. Trust me.

By the time we got within spitting distance of that star we'd worked out its habits; every time it spat at us we too were around the dark side of the place we'd come to know as Proximal. Proximal looks after Prime. That's just the way it was designed.

Okay, now there's someone I need you to meet. This here is a representation of my wife, Maria. Maria is/was one of my crew on the Neddermeyer and has manifested herself here before you to help with this orientation. Like myself she's moved on from the strictly human form, helped by the Proxie, but is appearing here as her old self for your... dammit, what is the word, I dunno, convenience? Comfort? To stop you going insane because you couldn't cope with seeing her in her current form? She is going to be passing amongst you handing out choice cards. You will see they are clearly marked A, B, and C, with a tick box alongside each. When you've decided which way you want to go just put a mark in the appropriate box.

Speaking of designed, I'd like you have a look at this for a moment.

(Hologrammatical 3-D representation of planetoid appears in middle of the auditorium.)

This is where we are. Look at it while I'm talking to you. Study it while I'm talking to you. You used to know every nanobyte of data on this map. I know that because I retrieved it from the database of your ship; this is what you've been studying for the last four weeks. Look at it closely. Three-quarter Earth sized planet. Ice at both the poles. Salt water seas. Two large island-shaped continents, not quite opposite each other but nearly, both straddling the equator. Several small islands dotted around. Couple of atoll reefs indicative of prior volcanic activity. Nitro oxygen atmosphere. Proper little paradise. No exterior evidence of intelligent life/civilisation/industrialisation. No poisonous chemicals in the atmosphere. No life-sapping ionising radiation. Small low-level carbon-based life forms in the sea and on the land. Photosynthesising carbon-based plants. If you'd written down what you were looking for before you came this is pretty much it, eh boys? How weird is that.

I need you to start remembering the details of your lives – who you were before you came here – what you wanted, what you liked – in order that you can choose wisely whom or what it is that you want to be next. One of the more unfortunate things about the lung worm from your current perspective – assuming that you opt for life continuance – is that whilst it is wiping out your ability to breathe it also exudes several potent neurotoxins that have the effects of closing down the human consciousness and translating one's 'soul' for want of a better word, into a state of what feels like perpetual Nirvana. In that respect it's a kindly execution; a swift and blissful death in which one is completely unaware one has actually died. Nevertheless, death has taken place. If you already know that 'death masquerading as perpetual Nirvana' sounds like your cup of tea, please tick box C now.

If you think you want to carry on "being" please carry on paying close attention to what I'm saying, try to remember your lives, and after listening to everything that I've said figure out whether option A or option B - or perhaps option C after all -would be your preferred end state.

Now, I'll tell you some more about what happened when we landed on this planet/moon – whatever the hell you want to call it. Hopefully some of your lives will come back to you while I'm doing this, then you can fill in the form, then I can get back to what it was I was doing before I was tasked with orienting you. We're going through the events of the past few weeks in the most detail because they are the key to recovering your longer term memories which are the key to recalling your core personality traits and formative experiences which will allow you to opt for box A, B, or C wisely, okay? What you've got to work out is, are you the sort of 'person' who wants a body or are you okay with moving on from being strictly human?

Like you, the first thing we did on coming into the system was make a beeline for this place. We parked ourselves around the safe side of the gas giant and entered a low orbit around this moon and started to marvel at what we saw. Three revolutions taking it all in, our jaws were still on the floor. This thing couldn't have got more beautiful if it'd tried. Both continents had so much going for them. I don't remember why but we ended up naming them Istanbul and Constantinople.

Istanbul stretched about thirty degrees to the north and fifty-five degrees to the south. The whole thing was shaped a bit like Africa from back home on Earth and like that continent the centre of this one seemed to be a vast shining desert. To the north the desert faded out into vast grassy plains and we could see small animals running there in huge herds. Going closer we could see they were two-legged leaping creatures about the size of domestic cats. The south of this continent seemed rocky and, as the desert petered out there, became populated by swarms of small hopping birds the size of puffins.

To the west of Istanbul there was a sizable island not so far off the coast. Further west from that were various random smaller islands.

Further west again Constantinople, a larger, more rounded continent, straddled the equator, forty degrees to the north and forty degrees to the south. Green and densely covered by something at the centre. To be honest we weren't sure if it was vegetation or rock but it rose up high; 500 feet, 1000 feet, 2000 feet in places. Impenetrable to our scanners and, when we flew over it, our eyes. Almost like a cityscape from Earth's past, low then towering incredibly high. Hundreds of square miles of this impenetrable green – is it vegetation? Is it rock? And then, again, a petering out of this uniformity, this green darkness, into plains of grassland and vegetation around the coast. And animals. Herds of animals the size of small ponies. It reminded me of sub Saharan Africa before the animals died. I'd only read of such things. We all had. I mean sure, I'd seen a few animals. But never simply "running around". Even the grunts wept.

We thought we'd better land. We thought we'd found paradise. We mapped it from orbit, scanned it 'til our databases were full and decided we'd head for Istanbul not Constantinople – primarily because the "ponies" running loose around Constantinople were sabretooth carnivores capable of ripping a man to sheds in seconds, judging by the way they efficiently and swiftly cleaned all the flesh from the bones of one of their comrades within minutes of it first looking up, forlornly incapacitated and stumbling, after breaking a bone in its leg.

ILADs aren't built for surface-jumping, as you know – indefinite warranty barring 'unforeseen circumstances' just travelling through inter-stellar space at one-tenth the speed of light – but surface jumping? That's another matter. That voids your warranty. That's what *shuttles* are for, right?? But hey, just because they weren't designed for it doesn't mean they can't do it. Just means they need a good goddamn service more often and do it too often without one and they might break. And besides, we only had a tiny two-man iShuttle and the scanners showed everything was A-OK and we'd come all this way and what could go wrong, right? We strapped in tight and Sam and Dodo pointed us at Paradise and we started to cut in through the atmosphere.

Got to love a good burn-through. All that initial heat and friction. Nothing quite like it. Makes you feel Alive! Two or three minutes of fire and flames and then we're scooting on over the waters, coming in on the coast of Istanbul fast at about 1800mph. Dark blue semi-night skies above us and a great big gas cloud swirly dark shadow planet "moon" blotting out three-quarters of the sky above us, glowing gold around the edges as the rays of Proxima Centuri shone through it from behind. Beautiful. There was "whooping" in the cockpit and the passenger-bay alike as we came in on that coast, all eyes to the view screens and tiny round 'port-holes'. Speed down to 500mph at a height of 1000 feet we were coming in slow to let Cartography do their thing when the skid started.

All at once, 1000 feet up, we hit something. Something like invisible ice preventing us going down further. And we became a hockey puck. Even the alarms on the alarms went off. Seat belts locked down tight pulling everyone back into their seats. Sam swore. D. wrestled with the controls. More lights than I knew our control board had went red. I heard my wife pray. We skidded, out-of-control, bouncing like a stone on some unseen sea, clean over Istanbul, now skimming waves on the other side at 500 feet, before skidding to a halt at the base of a mountain rising up on the far side of an island twelve miles to the west of the main continent. Inertial dampers broke our fall but the fall broke our back. This iLADS was never going anywhere again.

You'd have seen our ship when you landed. Still there. Albeit in two pieces. Three if you count the bubble universe. Although we're not quite sure where that went - we only know it wasn't in the hold after we crashed. One day we - or the Proxie - might find it, I guess. If you do step into it by accident at any point, whether in the body or out of it, please make sure to follow the usual protocols; remember to come to a halt the instant you realise you have entered another universe, remembering not to move your feet from their present location or to bring them together in any way, but to immediately bend, mark the point on the ground - with a marker of some kind, preferably indelible - and reverse your physical trajectory until you (hopefully) re-enter your originating universe where you will continue to mark the spot with said indelible marker and notify the authorities, taking care to guard the point of ingress until such authorities arrive to cordon the area off with full security and reality protocol.

When we landed we didn't land quite as neatly as you did. We dug a furrow eight to ten feet deep in the rich black dirt of the place we'd named Manhattan Island whilst orbiting above. Nice place, similar shape to Madagascar but a fraction of the size. One big mountain on the western coast. It'd been at the base of that we'd finally stopped our five mile out-of-control skid-and-scrape through the jungle there. We'd left our mark on the place alright. We cut right into it and made a big black scar across it. We'd been allowed to land there – if you can call it landing – as it wasn't inhabited. Not that we'd known that at the time. We thought we'd crashed. Which we had.

Apparently the Proxie had been telling us for weeks not to land, that the planet and the system were defended, that we weren't welcome. I thought I'd just been having a run of bad dreams that I couldn't remember when I woke up. A few of the others had been complaining of headaches, but there was nothing tangible. Some of you will have experienced the same thing. Try and remember if that's you because if that is, you have more options than some of your colleagues.

What we'd hit when we tried to land on Istanbul was their version of a defence shield. They call it the Rappel. Thus far and no further. Anything – craft or being – that tries to land here on Prime, unbidden or unwelcome will be forced to slide over the surface of the two main land masses, to rappel the inhabited places, and land on one of the designated landing pads either side of the main continents, dependent on their trajectory of entry. The Rappel will carry them to it and dump them there where they can live out the rest of their natural lives unharmed, unless identified as a threat to the Prox. In which case, natural termination by planetary intervention will occur.

Ladies, Gents and Inters, guess what. Planetary intervention is occurring. Mankind is a known contaminant and destructor of habitats. Our presence had been pre-programmed as 'undesirable' in this system for 400 or so Earth years, we were apparently warned not to come – did you get the message? Believe it or not, the Proxie had no idea we were practically STONE DEAF as well as stupid. Never underestimate the stupidity of Humanity. They know that now. Hence your compassionate options – which will also afford them the possibility of further study and potential evolution of the human brain beyond imbecile status. Nice to know your death is worthwhile, eh? Always look on the up-side.

We were more than an irritant. We were an antigen and we'd begun to provoke an immune response from the planet the second we spilled out of the sides of our gutted ship. Sitting on an upturned piece of fallen hull plate one of us bled into the dug up ground and a microbe in the soil, lying dormant, no heavier than a mould spore, became active to our DNA. And as it became active, it transmitted activation data to the dormancies in the soil around it. We started coughing before the end of the first shift, setting up Base Camp. By the end of second shift all attempts to do anything other than stay alive were abandoned and all resources were ploughed into Medical. By the end of third shift, eight of us were dead, twelve were in a coma and the rest of us? Coughing, coughing, coughing, and hallucinating. At least, I was.

I'd had this headache for so fucking long by then. It felt like forever. I shut my eyes against the pain for just one moment.

hello

On the inside of my skull. Or so it felt. What?

hello

you're dying

Uh, no shit, Sherlock.

sorry it took so long to get in touch

we didn't realise how ~~stupid~~ limited you are

your telepathic capacities are very small

in most of your crew they do not exist

will you let us help?

Hey, when you're dying and coughing up lung worms you might as well go with the flow, right? I said, sure! Started laughing and gave into the madness in my head. Ended up in a place quite like this one, only the Proxie I was talking to had only my morphined-up state of mind for reference and I found myself talking to a six foot tall white rabbit who would insist on calling me 'Alice' for the duration of the presentation. I had the same choice as you've got, Box A, Box B or Box C.

Let me tell you about the Proxie.

They come in two types. Loosely translated their names mean the Thinkers and the Do-ers. You can think of them as the bodied and the bodiless if you like, although that's not quite right. The Thinkers do have a physical form, of sorts. They're just not tied to it and they can change it from one thing to another. Or unhook their being from one corporeality and attach it to another, if they also choose. They can hitch a ride on someone else's body without displacing that someone. Although that someone does know they are there. Unless they choose not to tell. But I'm getting way off topic here. Thinkers would be Box A. If you picked Box A you'd no longer be human. You'd transcend your humanity; leave it behind. Move on from it. I did. Best thing I ever did. I can be anything I like. Go anywhere I like. Be anything I like. I can be a hydrogen atom in the heart of a star or experience a lightyear travelling as a transdimensional manifestation of infinite intent before manifesting briefly as a ... a Calabi–Yau manifold! – simply because !I can! – the ultimate statement of what we used to call God's creation, *being* to the fullness of *being* to the power of 'n.'

Box A. The ultimate freedom. Become a Type 1 Proxie. Morph. Evolve. Not open to all. The bad news is, even if you want this, only about one in ten of you has the option. The rest of you simply don't have the wherewithal for this to even be an option for you so. Tough luck there. Back on Earth the odds are about 1 in 100,000 in the general population so hey at least you know you're the cream of the crop even if you don't make it, ok? That headache you're feeling right now is the the Proxie probing your mental capacities. If you can see a green light in the front of your cerebral cortex, congratulations, you qualify. If you see a diffuse purple haze, bad luck there, your brain's not up to it. Can anyone see a green light? Let's see a show of hands. Oh, a fair few of you. Excellent!

If you've got the purple haze you'll notice Box A disappearing from your papers entirely right now -so you can't tick it by mistake. No need to tick box A yet if you've still got it, you might still want to opt for Box B. Or C.

Let me make it quite plain, even if you can opt for Box A

and you do opt for Box A you don't get to evolve, ascend, become a morphie, whatever you want to call it, right away. You've got to spend some time as a Box B type, being looked after by the type 2 Proxie for a while first, 'til you can learn what it takes to leave your body behind. Purple hazers you just don't have what it takes to do that, sorry. Your options are Boxes B and C only.

Okay.

Box B. The Do-ers. Type 2 Proxie. Ones with bodies. The other sort of Proxie. Well, they're… well they're a lot like us, in many ways. You remember that black mass on Constantinople; we couldn't work out if it was jungle or stone? Well, it was neither. That's their major city, on this planet at least. They're tall, slender, humanoid, bigger brained than us – gentle, graceful people. They live in harmony with their surroundings and with each other. They don't destroy their planets but live to service them and care for them and the local life forms, while exploring and appreciating the general space vicinity of wherever they're parked. Scientists, artists, artisans, they live like we did - in houses, in communities, exploring what it is to *be*. They live to serve. And they're willing to serve you. That's nice. Right?

The fact that you are being offered any sort of continuance at all is wholly down to these guys. So, be grateful. Mankind was long ago identified as a menace. We were given warnings not to come. We may not have got those warnings but Earth Govt did. Successive Earth Governments over several centuries. They sent us here anyway. Go figure. Hey, even Box C is nice. The Proxie are cool people. I've mentioned Box C already, haven't I? Death by Nirvana but you don't actually know you've died. There are far worse ways to kill a man, believe me.

But, it's not entirely out of the kindness and goodness of their hearts. Let me make this quite plain before we go any further. The Proxie are good but it will be a symbiotic relationship. They want something back. It's not completely straight forward. There'll be an element of give and take. This is a *two way*, mutually beneficial transaction they're proposing here.

First out, know this, they'll keep you alive. You'll be pain free and you'll be as happy as your personal psychology allows you to be in whatever psychological and emotional circumstances you choose for yourself . Medically speaking, they can't fix your lungs or kill off the worms and hey if they did you'd only breathe fresh ones in as the air is full of them. What they can do is neutralise the biotoxins the worms are giving off as they eat through your lungs – the ones that would otherwise send you to Nirvana - and then infuse oxygen into your tissues through the use of their own organic based technologies which will keep you alive and allow you to 'breathe' without your lungs. But, you'll be immobile. Keeping you alive means keeping you bound to a biobed. For life. That's the bottom line.

If you tick Box B, You will be completely dependent upon the Proxie for every facet of your daily lives. If you tick Box C, you'll be dead. Tough choice, eh?

Let me tell you more about your Box B lifestyle. You'll be held in zero-G or a fluid solution, to prevent bed-sores. By necessity, a hundred per cent immobile most of the time. Why is this better than death? Because your brain, your consciousness, *who you are*, will be linked into the Proxies' universal library where you will be able to live a Virtual Life in any way, shape or form you wish.

Many of the Prox's own children spend many hours of every day in there. There are whole worlds in there you can explore if you have a mind to or you can simply chose to inhabit a little patch of the Prox's cyberspace as yourself. Your own reality, shaped by your own mind, and interacting with others in there as you will. You'll be aware of your body but not confined to it and the Prox will take great care of you. They will consider it a great honour to have one of you entrusted to them. You could not be in safer hands.

The symbiotic thing? Yea, that's interesting. They've discovered they are partial to a variety of the fluids and bi-products a human body produces and they also have a great interest in our collective experiences. They're really keen on getting inside your mind and viewing aspects of your lives – kind of like an interactive experience. But it's fully consensual – sort of like being on a 'chat show' or having an interview with someone in Cyberspace. And of course, you get access to all their minds in exactly the same way, too – find out what it's like being a Proxie, from the inside. You'll share your experiences with them and they'll share their experiences with you and the sum of all knowledge will increase for everyone concerned.

In terms of the physical, whilst they're looking after your body – which they will take *great* care of - some bodily fluids will be harvested in a painless and harm-free manner, but this seems a small price to pay for the myriad of opportunities and knowledge and care they will be giving to us in return. Human bile has been found to have medicinal qualities that are useful to them so there will be a small drain attached to harvest this and similar fluids whilst you are in their care but this seems a small price to pay for what we're getting back and hey, anything to help them in return, right? Urine and other by-products are also collected and refined I believe. I'm given to understand the taste is agreeable to them and what they don't drink is utilised in some other way.

The expected lifespan of a human being kept in these conditions remains 120 years. Within the Virtual World you will be able to do whatever you want. Obviously you will have no sense of touch there, which you may find burdensome. The Proxie have promised they will work on that and hope to be able to give you a tactile projectable other 'self' at some point. Until then, there is only the virtual world for you. Those of you who are currently in bonded pair units they are willing to establish in bonded pair tanks if you so wish. If those of you who are not in bonded pair units do form emotional attachments whilst in the virtual world you may submit a request to form a bonded pair and be moved into a cohabiting tank. Recreational sexual activity will be possible, with care and reproduction may take place. There have been several births here already over the years. Of course, the child becomes infected with its first breath but that isn't a problem as the Proxie have become adept at caring for the needs of a human being both within the tanks and within their mainframe computers, no matter what its age.

Any other questions?

Please now select Box A, B or C as appropriate. Thank you.

Edited by Sam Taylor

FIRST CONTACT, LAST CONTACT

By CM Martin

The enormous alien ships started surrounding the planet at dawn Washington, D.C. time, Feb. 2, 2053. NASA and the World Space Association had been tracking them for nearly a week, ever since they'd entered the Sol System, but their arrival in Earth's orbit was damned inconvenient timing—not only was it Sunday, it was *Super Bowl Sunday.*

"Goddamn it anyway!" President-for-Life George Bush IV shucked off his Washington Redskins sweats and stalked over to his closet to pull out a blue suit, talking to himself as he often did. "Why the Hell do I have to dress up for E.T.? It's not like they're going to know who Armani is." Being President-for-Life was a pain in the ass; it was always cutting into his free time, and this crisis was no exception. When the first long-range telescopes had spotted the interstellar flotilla, the UN Security Council had promptly gone into session and by a vote of 14-1 (The United States being the one), they had decided that if the aliens requested a first contact, the *only* appropriate representative was President-for-Life Bush.

So now, instead of eating nachos and wings and watching grown men beat each other up over a ball, George had to get dressed up and climb aboard Air Force One to be ferried to Roswell, New Mexico. One of the alien ships had sent a message to NASA, requesting a meeting outside Area 51. This meant they knew there *was* an Area 51, and they probably knew it was chock-full of downed alien aircraft and the occasional extraterrestrial corpse. For more than 80 years, the official story had been that only drunks and lunatics actually believed in little green men, but as George had discovered when his grandfather was President, the U.S. government had known since 1947 that aliens were real. Now, the world was about to come face-to-face with them, and he, President-for-Life Bush, was the welcoming committee.

George swallowed nervously as he pulled in his gut in order to button his pants. This whole idea sucked. Sure, he'd seen *Close Encounters of the Third Kind*—but he'd also seen *Independence Day*. All the reports coming in agreed—the ships now in orbit were huge, sophisticated, and probably bristling with weapons. If these aliens were the equivalent of the ones in *Independence Day*, they'd easily blow the planet to Hell—and they might just start by vaporizing the reception committee.

Not for the first time, George Bush the IV cursed his father, his grandfather, and his uncle, all of whom had pushed him into a "life of public service"—or the easiest way to continue to steal shitloads of money for the clan, which was the real point.

"I never wanted to be President-for-Life," he muttered, adjusting his tie. "I wanted to be a bass player."

Air Force One landed on the long runway in the middle of a New Mexico desert. President-for-Life Bush disembarked, surrounded as always by a ring of Secret Service agents, and got into the limo that was waiting for him. The gaggle of Secret Service agents got in the next car; George's only companion (besides the driver) was his director of communications, Max Rocher. Max was a phenomenal liar, which made him the perfect communications director. Max had spent the flight in Air Force One's communications room, staying in touch with NASA, NATO, the Joint Chiefs, and the *National Enquirer,* the United States' leading newspaper since the demise of *The Star* four years before.

"Any updates?" Bush asked.

"Nothing new, sir. The aliens are sending the same message we've already received through a dozen different satellites, broadcasting it in English, Mandarin, Russian, Japanese, Arabic, Spanish, and French. They've apparently monitored our broadcasts for enough years to be fluent in all those languages."

"French?" George turned to stare at his flunkey. "Why the fuck would they be broadcasting in French?"

Rocher smirked. "Maybe they like snails or they want a good deal on a million cases of wine."

Despite himself, Bush chuckled. "Could be." He stared out the window, watching the desert roll by. "I wonder what they want."

"Maybe—maybe they're here to help," Rocher said hopefully. "Maybe they've got cures for cancer and global warming."

Bush snorted. "Yeah—and maybe they all ride unicorns and give away kettles full of gold. No, they want something, Max; you can bet on that. They want something from Earth, and I've got to be the one to tell them 'No.' Why me?"

"Well, you are the leader of the free world, sir," Max observed.

"Yeah, right. Tell that to the consortium of bankers who got that constitutional amendment through and made this job mine until I die. I'm a puppet, Max, Uncle Sam's puppet." Bush frowned and stared out the tinted window some more, wishing to hell he was back in the White House media room with a bucket of wings and about 20 cold beers, watching the Super Bowl as God intended.

Within 20 minutes, the limo arrived at Area 51, the largely secret, largely underground facility established in the early 1950s to study aliens and their artifacts (the people who did *Independence Day* had gotten that much right). Bush stepped out of his limo into blinding heat and a mass of people, every nerd in the place dressed up in a fresh lab coat, every soldier assigned to guard the fence crowding around to see the President-for-Life in the flesh.

"Sir." Major Younker, the base's commander, saluted. Bush returned it.

"Major," he said, "any word from our new friends?"

"Yes, sir," the major replied. "Their craft—some sort of shuttle, we believe—landed ten minutes ago; they have sent a message indicating they are waiting for your arrival."

"So no one's left the craft?'

"No, sir," the major replied. "They seem intent on waiting for you."

Bush fought down a surge of stomach acid that threatened to burn a hole right through him. "Well, then," he said as forcefully as he could manage with bile clogging his throat, "let's take me to their leader."

"This way, sir." Major Younker gestured. "Their craft is in our main parking lot." He grimaced. "They flattened nearly

70 cars—including my Prius."

The President had to fight back the sudden urge to laugh hysterically. The whole goddamned planet might be vaporized in the next ten minutes, and this desk jockey was worried about his fucking car?

"I'm...I'm sure the Federal government will offer some sort of compensation," Bush managed to say. *Assuming that there* is *a Federal government after today.*

"Um...yes, sir." Younker seemed to come to the belated realization that now wasn't the time to worry about getting help with his "the-aliens-smashed-my-auto" problem.

"Let's get this over with," Bush said.

"Yes, sir."

The alien's shuttle was as big as Air Force One—probably larger. *No wonder it took out 70 cars,* Bush thought as they approached. The craft was ringed by soldiers shipped in from the 523nd Airborne, but they were under strict orders not to make any hostile moves. Granted, Bush knew he could order a nuclear strike on the facility and blow the shuttle into its component atoms, but he had to assume that the aliens on the ground were in contact with the dozen mother ships overhead. Any aggressive action would guarantee Armageddon.

Gathered in a huddle at a further distance were representatives from the press, cameras recording and broadcasting this moment all over the world. Bush sincerely hoped that his last appearance in the media would not be as some alien ate his face.

The craft itself looked alien, but no more so than any Star Trek prop. It was somewhat square in shape, with four rather chunky-looking landing gears, one at each corner of the ship. It was a dull purple-gray in color, but it didn't look like it had been painted. Maybe whatever the material was, it was naturally that shade. There were no windows or ports that Bush could see, but he didn't have much time to examine the ship closely. Even as he and his cordon of Secret Service approached, there was a subdued "crack" and a hatch began to open in the side of the vehicle. The ring of soldiers guarding the craft shifted their feet, and Bush stopped, watching the opening widen. After a minute, some sort of ramp slid smoothly out of the craft and down to the pavement. The president waited for a few moments that seemed like an eternity, but there was no other sign of life. Bush turned to Shauna Maxwell, the head of his Secret Service detail.

"You and the others stay back," he said.

"Mr. President!" she protested, but Bush shook his head.

"Whatever's going to happen, you can't protect me from it," he said firmly. "I'm ordering you to stay here."

"Understood, sir," she replied, not looking at all happy about it. The president gave her a nod and then turned, moving across the open space and through the gate in the fence that surrounded the parking lot. Once inside, George took a few steps towards the alien's shuttle—and then he caught a flicker of motion inside the open hatchway. He stopped, and slowly, a figure emerged into the late afternoon sun, standing at the top of the ramp and looking around as cameras and iPhone 27s clicked and whirred.

There was no way to know if this alien was a member of the same race as the nine frozen corpses in Area 51's storage lockers, but having seen those bodies, George Bush V could tell that there were at least some racial similarities. Like the bodies from 1947, this alien was tall and slim, gray-skinned and apparently hairless, with a bulbous head, nostrils but almost no nose, a wide, lipless mouth, and huge, saucer-shaped black eyes. It was also naked, but it was apparently comfortable in that state. After a few moments, its gaze moved to the president, and Bush stepped forward, silently commanding his sphincter to stay clenched.

"On behalf of the people of Earth, welcome," he said, raising his voice as he did every time he addressed Congress.

Those ebony eyes looked at Bush for a long moment, and then the alien nodded and moved down the ramp. It had long, spindly-looking feet with four toes on each. As it moved, Bush watched, but he couldn't actually see those feet touch the ground. The alien glided across the blacktop, and now the president was certain its feet weren't touching the ground. It stopped about a yard in front of Bush and lifted one hand.

"As the representative of the Exploration Alliance, I greet you as well," it said. Its voice was slightly tinny, but neither high nor low-pitched enough to give a clue as to its gender—any more than its naked body did.

"Thank you, sir…um, ma'am?"

The alien didn't have eyebrows, but Bush got the distinct impression that if it had, one would have been raised.

"I see no relevance in that question, as we will not be indulging in mating rituals."

The president felt his face burning, but he managed to maintain his composure. "My apologies," he said. "How may I address you?"

"My name is Na'xil," the alien replied. "You are George Bush, the fourth of that name."

"I am," he replied. "I'm sorry, but you said something just a moment ago—the Exploration Alliance? Do you mean you represent more than one government, one world?"

"Indeed," Na'xil replied simply.

"So...there are more inhabited worlds besides yours?"

"George Bush, there are thousands of inhabited worlds," Na'xil replied. "My people have been exploring our galaxy for more than 600 of your years, but we have not yet discovered all the worlds that contain life. However, we are part of an alliance of nine worlds, nine cultures, all within our solar system. We have been monitoring your world and its people for the last 104 years; those who are our rulers decided it was time to make contact, so I have been sent here as their emissary."

"Of course, of course!" Bush said with a broad smile. He felt a thrill of excitement run through him. Now it all made sense. First contact, that's what it was called. These aliens wanted Earth to join them in exploring the galaxy. They had to have incredible technology, and if they were civilized enough to form into scientific alliances for stellar exploration, they'd probably be willing to share their knowledge with new members. Maybe they *did* offer a cure for cancer and global warming!

"And we are delighted to welcome you. Would you like to

go somewhere more comfortable? I mean, we can adjourn to a conference room, and perhaps you would like some Earth food and water, and then we can discuss how we might benefit your alliance."

But Na'xil shook its head. "That will not be necessary," the alien replied precisely. "I will not be on your planet much longer."

"But…I don't understand," Bush said. "Surely there are matters to discuss, diplomatic relations, treaties, a sharing of knowledge…"

The lipless mouth twitched slightly in what might have been amusement. "I believe you misunderstand my purpose here," Na'xil said calmly. "I have been sent as an emissary to let the people of Earth know that by decree of the Exploration Alliance, this system is going into quarantine."

"Quarantine?"

"Yes," the alien being replied. "As I said, we have been observing you—and to be blunt, we are horrified by what we have seen. As a species, you spend much of your time fighting one another and over the most trivial cultural differences. You do not care for your poor, your aged, or even your young in many cases. You have all but exhausted your planet's natural resources, and even though those who rule your people know this, their greed is such that they do nothing to stop the damage. Worst of all, those few noble institutions humans created, be they devotion to gods or the philosophic practice you call democracy—these have been perverted and their value lost." Na'xil looked at him with what George Bush IV fancied was contempt in its gaze.

"Life is sacred to us, even inferior life," it continued. "So we will not destroy your planet and its people. We will simply contain you, as one might contain a wild and dangerous beast. Perhaps in a hundred generations, your people will be civilized enough to join the universe." The alien turned to go.

"But…you…you can't do that!"

Na'xil's head swiveled towards Bush. "Actually, we can," it replied. "You see, Mr. President-for-Life, there is only one scientist currently on your planet who is even close to discovering the secret of faster-than-light space travel. His name is Professor Cochrane. We have been in communication with him and have offered him a home among us. He was delighted to accept. So you see, you will not be able to leave the Sol system for many hundreds of years. As I said, perhaps that will be time enough." Na'xil paused. "Oh, and we are taking the French."

"What???" Bush's eyes bugged out of his head.

"Yes, they are the only truly civilized culture you humans have produced. We have informed them we have plenty of vineyards and caves in which to make blue cheese. They are bringing their own snails. Farewell, George Bush. Let us hope you and the other humans are content in this squalid nest you have created—until the day when you can finally evolve sufficiently to join us."

The Exploration Alliance was as good as its word. Its members left the Earth in strict quarantine for precisely 523 years before sending another envoy.

By then, of course, the apes had taken over.

WOLFIE

By Sam Taylor

Dale Bryce looked down. That was supposed to be a mistake, but he actually found it a thrill. The deep U-shaped scar left in the mountainous landscape by the long-melted glacier dropped away below him. He dangled near the top on two ropes, one knotted around his hips like a harness, the other feeding through it past several shiny carabiners and hanging down below him for about fifty feet. He took a moment to look up the lush glacial valley into the misty green-blue distance, then turned his attention back to what he was doing.

Climbing down a thousand foot precipice using a hundred foot rope might seem ill-thought-out to some, but Dale had carried that hundred foot rope rolled on his shoulder for twenty miles through rugged terrain. The weight of that much rope was bad enough; there was no way he could have carried more. So the cliff would be tackled in stages, traversing fifty feet at a time, finding or making anchor points after each traverse and dropping the rope another fifty feet. It was tedious work, but not as tedious as the climb up the other side of the deep-cut valley would be, anchoring the rope with every foothold upwards.

Still, the view was spectacular. The old scar of the glacier had cut a swathe through the rocky landscape long ago, before the climate changed. Since then the greenery had grown to cover almost every inch of the now sub-tropical landscape with shrubbery, moss or trees. Even on the bare cliff face the occasional tree had managed to establish itself, a miracle of twisted roots embedding themselves into the bare rock. Dale knew to avoid those places though. Sometimes the tree roots stabilised the area where they were growing, but in other cases the roots split the rocks deep within and left the whole cliff face around the tree unstable; and it was impossible to tell which. Dale had seen one man plummet to his death in a shower of debris after anchoring his rope to such an unstable tree. The whole tree had gone with him, and quite a few tonnes of rock.

He bounded down the rock face, the familiar buzz and whine of the ropes through the carabiners the only noise apart from the occasional bird call. He pulled his rock hammer out of his utility belt, and hammered three pitons into the solid rock. The 'ting, ting' of the metal hammer on the metal pins seemed loud in the clear air. He hammered another pin in at foot height and stepped on it, holding one of the top pins, then used a small loop to connect his harness to one of the other pins. Then he freed himself from the rope and gave two emphatic tugs on the rope.

He looked up and waited. Terry York's pale face peered over the edge of the cliff-top. "What?" she called, sounding nervous even at this distance. All his crew had baulked at the top of the thousand-foot drop, and even tough old Jim Davis had flat refused to make the descent. Dale was annoyed, because going down the glacier and up the other side would save them about three weeks of hiking time. Hiking through territory with wolf-bears would probably cost him the lives of one or two of his team.

He called back, "You coming down, York, or you gonna stand there all day?"

There was no answer, but in a minute, the ropes beside him flapped and rolled, and he smiled. York was on her way down.

He looked up to see her butt and legs splayed out awkwardly, like a human spider crawling down the wall. She tried a few bounces out and back, and Dale smiled. York was a trouper. He waited and watched.

Eventually she arrived at the end of the rope, breathless and big-eyed and clinging instinctively to him. "Wow! That's fun!"

The rope swung her close to him and he grabbed her for a quick kiss, leaving her even more breathless and smiling broadly. The kiss did not hold her attention for long though, as she looked anxiously down, "What now?"

"We bring the rope down and go again," he smiled at her inexperience.

"How? Just ask Davis to undo it at the top?" she wondered dubiously. "Won't it land on us?"

Dale nodded approvingly, "That's what I like about you, Terry, you actually think. No, we leave the anchors and set the rope up to feed down through them for the next traverse. At the bottom I'll show you what a hundred feet of rope landing on the ground sounds like and you'll understand just why we don't let it go. I've seen three men killed by being knocked off cliffs by ropes they've released above them."

"Wow. You must hang around a lot of stupid people, boss," she grinned.

Dale loved her at that moment more than ever. He grinned, and replied, "I like it that you get me."

She laughed, and they turned their attention to bringing the rope down the cliff face and resetting it on the pitons for the next run downwards.

Bryce went first again, rappelling in a series of confident bounds down the cliff. York clung to the anchorage point above him and watched.

They worked their way pass by pass down the enormous cliff, until they only had one pass to go, of about forty feet.

Bryce was enjoying himself. He knew York was watching and couldn't resist the urge to show off a little. He pushed off harder and took a huge swing downwards, then braced himself for the impact on the rock below. His boots hit the rocks, and suddenly everything went wrong. Instead of bouncing off the rock face, his feet plunged inwards through a thin shell of rock and with a shout of dismay he went straight through the cliff face, scraping and scratching his arms and shoulders on the sharp, thin rock edges as they shattered.

He landed in a confusion of rubble and cursed vehemently as the rope burned his wrist, but he managed to land without injuring himself any further and looked about curiously. He heard yelling from outside the cave, and suddenly a tug on the rope alerted him to the fact that York was coming down. She arrived within seconds. Fast learner indeed, he thought.

"Dale! Dale!" she cried, then looked at him standing in the cave staring at her.

"Oh, you're fine. Of course you're fine," she grumbled.

"I'm always fine. Stop being such a girl," he admonished as she ran up. He turned to look into the cave.

A sudden crack over the back of his head reminded him not to tease anyone who was holding lots of small metal climbing devices. "Ow!"

"Asshole!" she said, and disentangled herself from the rope eagerly, looking in the cave, "What do you think is in here? Look, there's a corridor."

"I wasn't planning to explore it."

"We have rope," she pointed out. "We can go in as far as we like and find our way out."

"We have a cliff face to climb down, a river to cross, and only a limited number of daylight hours."

"Oh God, you're boring sometimes!" she exclaimed.

He sighed, stung by her remark although he didn't show it, "Well…"

"Come on, Dale, it'll be fun! We might find something interesting."

He looked up grimly, "These caves may not be stable, Terry. I mean there's a hole here, this cave. How many other holes are there? The whole internal structure of this cliff-face might be unstable. Especially with the lakes all around up above."

"It's solid rock, Dale. You worry too much." She strode off into the darkness, lifting a light-ball in front of her as she left him behind.

"Terry!" He shucked the ropes, but stopped to jam the rope into a crevice to hold it inside the cave, then moved quickly after her. He saw her waiting for him up ahead, silhouetted by the small light-ball in the dark depths of the cave, and walked up grumbling, "You really should know better than to go wandering off like this. If we get much further into this…."

He stopped, confused, when she neither responded nor turned to look back at him. He walked up behind her and put a hand on her shoulder, but her name froze on his lips as he felt the rock-like tension in her shoulder. He looked into the dimness over her shoulder and as his eyes adjusted to the lower light, saw what had stopped York in her tracks; a huge female wolf-bear, sitting occupying most of the width of the tunnel they were peering into, crouched to pounce and angrily eyeing the light source in York's hand.

The creature's shoulders were a foot higher than Bryce's head, and it had a powerful build. It looked for all the world like a cross between an oversized timber wolf and a Kodiak bear, which is where the name wolf-bear came from. It was generally accepted that the creatures had been the result of either genetic engineering during the madness of the DNA Wars, or were some sort of mutation or crossbreed that had occurred in the aftermath of the Great Nuclear War seven centuries ago. No one would ever likely know. Most records of that time had been destroyed in the war.

The wolf-bear's lip was curled savagely back from a row of sharp teeth gleaming in the darkness as its muscles bunched under thick black fur, tensing ready to pounce on York.

Bryce shoved her aside and pushed her back behind him, drawing his disruptor and firing in one swift movement. He stood stunned as the disruptor beam reflected off something between them and the wolf-bear female. The beam ricocheted irregularly off the cave wall, coming back past Bryce and narrowly missing his ear. He heard York swear behind him. At the same time, the wolf bear female launched viciously at Bryce with snake-like speed…. then struck something between itself and Bryce, smashing its face onto an invisible barrier.

Bryce's heart, when it finally stuttered back to beating at all, began hammering as the wolf-bear slavered viciously across the invisible barrier. The creature bloodied its mouth and broke two massive teeth on whatever it was that Bryce could not see. He realised his hand was being grasped in a vice-grip by York, who looked wide-eyed over his shoulder at the slavering monster.

"What the hell?" she managed to ask in an oddly squeaky voice.

"There's some sort of barrier," said Bryce breathlessly.

"That's lucky," she said.

"Lucky doesn't even begin…." Bryce hesitated, seeing the wolf-bear female begin to dig enthusiastically at the tunnel wall beside whatever the barrier was. As she moved to the side, two puppies came into view, about the size of Alsatian dogs, but with their big round eyes and rounded ears, obviously only a couple of months old. They looked a little sleepy and confused.

York asked, "Do you think she'll get through?"

"What the hell is that?" asked Bryce, poking a cautious finger at the invisible barrier.

"I don't know, but Bryce…" their heads both snapped up as they heard an odd crack from just above where the wolf-bear was scrabbling at the tunnel wall.

"Let's get out of here!" yelled Bryce, as they heard another crack and water began gushing into the tunnel above the wolf-bears. He grabbed York's arm and heard the puppies yodel with terror as he turned to hustle her towards the light from the opening of the cave.

Suddenly something hit Bryce on the head from above, and he put a hand up to protect himself… only to cut himself on a sharp edge. With a roar, the tunnel wall and roof gave way and Bryce and York were thrown on the ground next to a stunned looking black wolf-bear puppy. Bryce looked up into a wall of water and flying rubble and grabbed onto anything he could, but whatever they were on seemed slippery, like glass. He found an edge and clung on, with

York's arms around his waist, as they were swept out of the cave as the whole cliff face below them subsided under a wall of water. York screamed as they found themselves surfing down the remainder of the cliff face towards the river rapids below on some sort of near-invisible, spinning bowl. In the melee, one of the wolf-bear puppies had ended up on the invisible surface with them.

The wolf-bear puppy scrabbled for purchase on the slippery surface, but as they spun it yelped again as it was flung around and further towards the rim of the bowl. It slid past Bryce with a terrified look in its huge brown eyes. Its back legs slid over the edge of the bowl when they were still twenty metres above the jagged rocks below, and it whined as it slid further and further towards the edge. It looked imploringly at Bryce, who suddenly reached out and grabbed a handful of the puppy's fur and held it on the bowl. It managed to scrabble its back end back onto the bowl and crouched down and gave him a look which he could have sworn was gratitude. His hand was millimetres from the deadly jaws, but the puppy just stared at him and did not open its mouth.

There was a feeling of falling then a swift sense of deceleration as the body of water struck the rocks and was deflected back up to cushion their descent. By some miracle they bounced thrice more and then were in the river, slowing down as the water from the cliff face was absorbed by the flow of the river. Bryce looked back and caught a glimpse of the wolf-bear female and the other cub, lying twisted and broken on the rocks behind them. He heard a whimper from beside him and saw the puppy looking back at its dead mother.

They floated down the river, clinging to the glass-like bowl, and eventually the bowl floated to the edge of the river and into a small round eddy pool where it circled up against the bank. Bryce handed the exhausted York up onto the bank, then turned and looked down at the wolf-bear puppy. It tried to reach the edge, but whimpered as the edge of the bowl dipped down, and retreated towards the middle again, unable to gain purchase with its paws.

Bryce sighed and swore, "Shit." He grabbed the sharp edge of the strange flat bowl, and held it up with both hands, then looked up at the wolf-bear puppy, "Come on."

The puppy took a cautious step towards him, then another. It made it to the edge of the bowl and leapt up onto the bank. Bryce released the bowl and turned to stare straight into the eyes of the most vicious creature of the northern wilderness. The puppy was small compared to an adult wolf-bear, but it was bigger than any dog or wolf on the planet, and its jaws were already big enough to tear Bryce's head off. It opened those huge jaws, and Bryce stared at gleaming white, needle sharp puppy teeth, each as long as Bryce's index finger. He was close enough to see yellow and blue flecks in the irises of the puppy's brown eyes. Bryce stared intently at the expression in those eyes.

York slowly drew her disruptor from her belt, but Bryce held up a hand. The puppy's eyes slipped sideways to watch her, as she stopped raising the disruptor York stared incredulously at them both, then her eyes slid back to survey Bryce. The jaws opened a little wider, pulling the black lips back into what looked like a snarl.

Then a huge, pink tongue swiped wetly across Bryce's face. He flinched, then opened his eyes and looked at the puppy.

"Well, I'll be damned," he whispered, and slowly reached out a cautious hand to rub gently behind the surprisingly soft ears. The puppy's tail began to wave slowly back and forth, and Bryce began to grin. "Good boy."

He was swiped several more times with the wet tongue, then the puppy just stood looking at him. He said, "Well, that was a quick descent."

He looked up. York was still staring at him and the puppy. Bryce asked, "What?"

"If you back away slowly, I can get a clear shot at it."

"Don't you dare hurt him!"

Her mouth dropped open, "You are not seriously thinking of... what are you thinking of? Keeping him? Dale, no!"

"Oh, come on, York, he's a baby for Christ's sake."

"He's a wolf-bear, Dale. A wolf-bear."

Bryce nodded, "Could come in handy as a guard dog."

"Could eat us in our sleep tonight, too."

"I don't think so."

She glared at him stubbornly.

Bryce turned to look at the bowl he was still holding on to. "Get over the dog, Terry. What the hell is this bowl thing?"

York turned her attention to the strange, glass-like bowl that the swirling water flow was helping to keep against the bank, "I have no idea."

"And what was it doing buried almost a thousand feet deep in solid rock? Geologically, that makes it about a million years old."

"It can't be. It's not even scratched."

He gave her a look. Beside him, the puppy sniffed at the bowl and growled at it as it bobbed in the water. All the dirt and stones had spun off it as they fell, and the water had washed it clean underneath. It sparkled like newly made glass in the sunlight, the water under it making unusual, swirling patterns through which they had a clear view of the rocks the bottom of the pool.

Bryce tugged at it and frowned, "It's not glass. It would have shattered. And besides, it's way too light. I think I can lift it out of the water."

He tugged harder, and gradually, in eerie silence, pulled the flat, glass-like bowl structure out onto the bank. The puppy backed up growling beside him.

Bryce shook his head and stared at it. "It's perfectly clean."

They both stood back and stared at it. York whispered, "What is it?"

The puppy tilted its head and sat beside Bryce, staring at

the object. Bryce felt a nudge under his hand and patted the puppy's head.

"Well, what a day," he said. "I wonder how long it will take Davis to get down here?"

"I don't know. I wonder if he even knows we got in trouble. Odd that he hasn't called on the radio."

Bryce frowned and thumbed open the radio case on his belt. He pulled out some flattened and broken pieces of metal and plastic, and said, "That's why. Damn!"

York stepped away a little to get a better view of the cliff face they had descended, York and the wolf-bear puppy following.

York laughed and pointed. There, already half-way down the cliff-face following their line of descent, were a dozen ant-like figures rappelling down rapidly. "On his way."

"They must have heard the roar of the avalanche from up top. Jim did say he was going to wait until we got across the valley safely."

Bryce and York settled down on the rocks to wait, the huge wolf-bear puppy sitting at Bryce's feet.

York said, "He really seems to have taken to you."

"He's not stupid," grinned Bryce, and patted the puppy, which gave him a friendly paw.

"I wonder if they're all like this when they're young," she pondered.

"Not from what I've heard. Born vicious, is what people say."

"I wonder what's different about this one?" persisted York.

"Maybe it's because I saved his life?"

York laughed softly, "Gratitude? That would imply a level of intelligence."

"Maybe he's smarter than the average wolf-bear," said Bryce.

She gave him a long look, "Maybe. Or maybe he's still in shock from the fall and he'll turn on us when he recovers."

Bryce pursed his lips and looked at her, then at the wolf-bear. He found himself hoping she was wrong.

They waited as the light lowered and the evening descended slowly. Eventually they heard voices as Jim Davis and his team followed the trail of debris downstream. Bryce called out, "Hello!"

"Hello!" called back a voice, and soon their team caught up with them, a slightly pale looking Davis in the lead. He froze when he saw the wolf-bear puppy standing at Bryce's side. "What the hell, Dale?"

"We picked up a stray. He's fine. Just a pup."

Davis walked up cautiously, staring at the wolf-bear and the strange, round, flattened bowl of something that looked like glass, that his captain was standing beside. He stood silent for a moment, and said, "Well, this should be a good story. I assume you're both okay, no broken bones or anything?"

"Yup, fine," grinned Bryce, and Davis shook his head. "You would be."

He looked at the wolf-bear at Bryce's side, and added, "You should shoot the wolf-bear and dump it in the river."

"Hey! No!"

"Dale," Davis waited until Bryce looked at him, and went on, "York and Chensky can smell a wolf-bear fifty miles away. How are they supposed to do that when there's one already in the camp and the place is full of their scent?"

"Shit."

To Bryce's surprise, York spoke up, "Leave the puppy alone."

Davis and Bryce looked at her. She went on, "He's different. They all have an individual scent. Isn't that right, Chensky?"

"What? Oh, yes."

Davis looked dubious still, but Bryce said, "That's settled then. The puppy stays with us."

"Great," muttered Davis, and turned to start directing the rest of the team to set up camp.

Bryce sat up late, worrying about what York had said

about the wolf-bear puppy. To his surprise, the puppy carefully stepped onto the strange bowl and walked unsteadily over to settle down to sleep in the middle of it, curling its long tail over its nose. Bryce climbed onto the bowl and joined it. The puppy must have been putting out a lot more body heat than he realised, because it seemed warm in the centre of the bowl. Bryce sat with his back against the puppy and worried about whether he had done the right thing in rescuing and adopting the pup. He was asleep in minutes.

Bryce awoke the next morning with a pair of huge brown eyes looking at him expectantly. He sat up and rubbed his eyes, and looked around. He was still in the bowl, the rest of the team scattered around on the rocks still sleeping. Chensky gave him a wave from his watch position above on the rocks. Bryce sighed and got up and scrambled to a secluded point to relieve himself. The wolf-bear puppy followed him, waited until he had finished then squatted down and peed exactly where Bryce had. He shook his head at it, washed his hands in the river, then looked up sharply as the wolf-bear puppy lay down on the river bank and dipped its front paws in the water just as he had. Bryce stared at it, as it then turned around and dipped each back paw in the water, swooshing it from side to side as Bryce had done with his hands.

A quiet voice beside Bryce murmured, "Anyone would think the damned thing was intelligent."

Bryce turned to look at Jim Davis. "Just because it imitates me? I don't know. Maybe we humans tend to see imitative behaviour as a sign of intelligence, because it's something we do. It's not necessarily so, though, Jim."

Suddenly the wolf-bear puppy turned and disappeared at that lightning fast, silent run that had been the end of many an unsuspecting soldier. Bryce and Davis spun around to silence. They waited for a few minutes, then Davis asked with a frown, "He gone then?"

Before Bryce could answer, the puppy returned with a small deer in its jaws, walked up to Bryce, and dropped it at his feet.

Bryce hesitated, then grinned and cautiously petted the puppy on the top of its jet black head. "Good boy!" He turned to Davis and smiled, "Breakfast!"

"Damn. This little fella could be handy," mused Davis, then looked at the wolf-bear puppy and added, "Couldn't you, Wolfie?"

Bryce was a little annoyed that the name stuck. He had been vaguely tossing over ideas for names in his mind. But Wolfie it was.

They banked up the fire and sliced up the deer, giving about half the animal to Wolfie and trying to ignore the crunch and crack of bones and flesh as the puppy ate at Bryce's side.

They headed upstream to have a look at the place where they had fallen, and Bryce decided to stay for a few days when they found some odd black circular objects, smaller than the original big clear flattened bowl that had saved their lives, but similarly light in weight.

He got Davis and a few of the men to help him push Wolfie's mother and littermate into the river before they began to rot. Wolfie sat beside him watching the bodies float away until they were out of sight, then pushed his head against Bryce's side, giving a small lost whimper. Bryce petted him gently.

In a few days the soldiers grew used to the black form at Bryce's side, and Bryce grew used to having a warm, black body curled at his feet every night. Davis had found more black shapes buried in the cliff face or scattered down on the rocks below where they had fallen. There were more circles, some blocks, ovals and a few odd shapes, all made of the same kind of smooth, black obsidian-like substance.

After a few days they set the shapes out on the rocks. They stared at the scattered items, and Bryce said, "I wonder if it was some sort of boat? It could have fallen down the cliff?

"And got buried in solid rock how?" asked York, ever the

logical one.

Bryce scratched his head. He walked over to the glass bowl that they had first found, and tugged at it experimentally. Beside him, Wolfie's ears pricked up and he tried to help, dragging the bowl with his teeth.

Bryce cut himself and swore, and after giving his hand a quick lick, Wolfie mouthed at the bowl again and dragged it determinedly towards a section of black.

"Leave it Wolfie," suggested Bryce. "You'll only cut yourself."

Wolfie "ruffed" at him through his teeth and dragged the two pieces together until they almost touched, then raced back to Bryce and turned to look at his work.

Bryce sighed and went to turn away, but suddenly heard a humming sound. He turned back to stare, as the glass bowl slowly glowed blue, then rose up off the ground and hummed. The black piece turned over slowly and moved towards the bowl, and then there was a red flash as the two seemed to unite along one edge. Gently the combined pieces settled back onto the ground.

"What is this, some sort of puzzle?" asked Davis. Bryce shook his head.

"I think it's self-assembling," suggested young Chensky. "They had stuff like that." Chensky was a history buff.

"How'd the fucking dog know that?" demanded York.

"Oy!" protested Bryce, and Wolfie gave her a long look, then trotted over to another piece of the scattered objects, and dragged it towards the first two.

"Dale, what if it's a bomb?" warned Davis, looking worried.

That stopped Bryce in his tracks. After a few minutes of heated debate, he told them that anyone who wanted to leave could, but wouldn't get a cent of the proceeds if it turned out they were onto something lucrative.

Davis grinned as they all opted to stay. Wolfie kept finding pieces to drag to the front of the bowl, and gradually the egg-shaped black object took shape. Wolfie's tail was wagging enthusiastically now, and even Bryce felt a little bit excited. Whatever this was, it was pretty high-tech, and that meant money.

"It's a boat!" said Chensky.

"Looks like it would handle the rapids pretty well," mused Davis, watching the large, egg-shaped black form take shape.

"It'd have to be powered," added York, as another piece glowed and it floated up into the air, then snicked smoothly into place. "Look at the way those pieces are glowing and rising up."

Bryce was looking excited, "If it's a boat that can handle these rapids, imagine the time that will save us in hiking! Our prospecting would be ten times more efficient."

They stood around the objects as they gradually all came together and made up a perfect black egg shape with a shiny windscreen made of the bowl that had originally saved Bryce and York from Wolfie's mother.

To Bryce's delight, the egg shape righted itself with the windscreen facing upstream and hovered a couple of inches off the ground. He walked around it, and asked, "How do we get in?" Wolfie walked at his side, sniffing at the shiny black sides of the object, until suddenly there was a sharp hiss and a circular door opened at waist level to Bryce. Wolfie sniffed curiously then jumped in, and Bryce climbed up after the wolf-bear pup. Davis, York and the Chensky brothers were quick to follow, their curiosity getting the better of them.

"It's as big as a house!" exclaimed Davis.

Bryce walked up and stared out the windscreen. At his feet was a strange circular pad, about a metre across. Davis walked up beside him and said, "Odd. No chairs."

Wolfie sniffed at the pad and sat happily down on it. Then the door snicked shut with a soft thud that sounded very final. Bryce and Davis jumped.

"I don't like this," said Bryce. "Let's see if we can get that door open."

The Chensky brothers moved up with York and started

fiddling around at the walls, feeling around for any sort of control mechanism. Davis went to where the door had been, but could find no trace of it. Davis said, "That's a helluva seal."

York looked up with sudden comprehension. "It's a submarine! It's not just a boat!"

"Ohhh," said the Chensky brothers in unison, and Bryce gave them an odd look.

Bryce pointed out, "You'd hardly need submarine capability for these shallow rapids. Maybe it was designed else-"

Suddenly Norm Chensky interrupted him, "Hey! I think I found the accelerator!"

And suddenly, green mountaintops flashed downwards outside the windscreen. Then there was blueness. Then the blueness gave way to a flash of light, then darkness. Then Bryce could see the stars, very clear and bright, outside the windscreen.

Bryce's eyes slid from side to side. Everyone froze in place. Then the yelling started.

Davis uttered something that sounded vaguely religious when he turned and saw the view outside the windscreen. York was swearing up a storm of profanities.

Then Davis said, "Fuuuu-uck."

They all turned to the windscreen, or, as it turned out, view screen.

There, serene in a black velvet star field, lay the unmistakeable, lapis, verdant green and white globe of Earth.

It was shrinking.

Bryce was the first to recover his wits and snap out, "I want control of this vessel, NOW."

"Doing our best, sir," gasped Norm Chensky.

Davis stepped slowly up beside Bryce and they stood staring transfixed at the shrinking Earth. "Oh, Jesus, Dale, you've done it this time!" said Davis.

"Fuck." Bryce looked frantically about the vessel, "What the fuck is this? Where is it taking us?"

Davis looked around too. "I don't know. All I know is, I don't like the idea of being taken somewhere I don't want to go by someone who puts a bloody dog-bed in the middle of their space ship bridge, for Christ's sake!"

Bryce frowned and was about to say something, when Chensky said, "I think I have something, sir! Some sort of ancient ship's log. I'm guessing the vessel is operating on autopilot, maybe taking us back where it came from. I'll play the log, and maybe we can get an idea of what whoever owned this ship originally looked like."

Bryce was looking at him, then turned as he heard Wolfie whine and saw the dog look up at what they now realised was a view screen. On the screen, turning to look at them, was the ages-old image of a great, black-furred creature, clad in metal armour with what looked like a disruptor at its belt. It turned and gazed at them, and Bryce felt a vice tighten around his chest as he saw the frightening intelligence in the dark liquid eyes of an adult, male wolf-bear.

Wolfie wagged his tail and whimpered hopefully.

The image, obviously degraded, faded and the screen went blank.

The ship rocketed on towards its destination.

"Nice doggy," said four voices in unison.

Edited by Sam Taylor

MORE EXCELLENT READS FROM SGA:

More info at *www.sgapublications.com/our-books.php*

Tales from the Perseus Arm (Volume I)

The stunning first volume of science fiction stories from a small group of hand-picked new authors chosen from over 3,000 writers from the US, UK, Ireland, Germany and Australia, plus some award-winning professionals writers!

Deadly Jewel by Sam Taylor

Zokar Rizian is a cold-blooded murderer and a self-seeking scavenger. But in committing an unexpected act of friendship, he becomes an unlikely hero, and is forced into an uneasy alliance to protect a planet that nobody else thinks is worth saving – Earth.

The Eye of Shiva (sequel to Deadly Jewel) by Sam Taylor

Shiva Kiran and Zokar Rizian are living in a changed galaxy. The Galactic Union is rebuilding its fleet, led by a furious Empress hell-bent on revenge.

Natira, Child of the Clouds by CM Martin

A young woman called Natira, struggling to stay alive using her talents as a thief and a harlot, has no idea that she has the power to topple a monarchy.

Dissolution by Debbie Painter

In a world gone inexplicably wrong, Peter Ogden is torn between love and duty, past and future, as he feels greatness slipping from his grasp.

Edited by Sam Taylor

ABOUT THE AUTHORS

Patricia Burn, (Cover art and story The Trouble with Coughing)

Patricia has an Honours Degree in both Politics and Literature and has been many things to many people. A polymath with an altruistic streak she is at her happiest listening to music whilst creating new artwork. Also runs a Rattery. Has been known to talk to God.

John Gribbin (Easy as Pi)

John Gribbin studied astrophysics in Cambridge, then worked for Nature and New Scientist. He writes science fiction based on fact, and science fact that reads like fiction. He also writes songs for the group "Three Bonzos and a Piano". His latest book Timeswitch is now available on Kindle and in print at http://www.amazon.com/Timeswitch-John-Gribbin-ebook/dp/B00I0F7898

Steve Guest (What the Hell is This For; Where Did We Come From?)

A multidisciplinary individual, with little or no discernible discipline. A science trained nurse and counsellor, fixer of all things, framer, aquarist, graphic artist, computerizer, wannabe musician. Lately; writer of excellent and terrible poems and short stories. Next, not sure, but his readers hope it's more of his 'quirky' writing.

Rachael Kelly (Wavelength)

Rachael won an Aspiring Novelist award in Ireland in 2014 with her novel 'Edge of Heaven.' She has a PhD in film theory and a mild obsession with Marcus Antonius, and her first non-fiction book (which featured both of these things) was published in 2013.

Salvatore B Lombard (Little Ghost of Elvis)
A Classics student who enjoys studying language, Salvatore spends his free time doodling cartoons and picking up horse poop.

Tim McLean (Time Will Tell)
2014 continues to be an exciting year for T M McLean (Tim to his friends); not only does he have several short stories due for publication, but Tim's debut children's book, The Sword of Gomar, will be released later in 2014 and he is busy editing several anthologies including 'Fear's Accomplice' for NoodleDoodle Publications and KnightWatch Press.

Visit www.facebook.com/noodledoodlepub or http://noodledoodle.tk for more details.

C. M. Martin (Asylum, First Contact – Last Contact)
When not writing, teaching, crafting or plotting world domination, Martin fulfils her destiny as the indentured servant of four cats and two ferrets. Her first novel Natira, Child of the Clouds, is now in print and is available from SGA via Amazon: http://www.amazon.com/Natira-Clouds-Stormcaller-Series-Volume/dp/0987320289

Debbie Painter (Robby)
A graduate of the University of Tennessee Knoxville, Debbie was employed for many years by the State of Tennessee. Upon retirement, she is trying a new field – writing. Her first novel 'Dissolution' was published on 9 March 2014 and is available from Amazon: http://www.amazon.com/Dissolution-Debbie-Painter/dp/1496196279

Kate Welty (Influence, Travelers)

Kate's real life, her passionate internal life, has always leapt and wept, laughed and stormed within the fictions of other writers' stories; there she lived joyfully within their realities. Now, inexplicably, she is creating stories. Perhaps that is good. It is certainly interesting.

Sam Taylor (Editor, and story Wolfie)

Sam Taylor, the driving force behind Perseus, is an Australian science fiction author who has a science degree and manages to happily ignore that fact. Sam rehabilitates and rides horses, has been shot at occasionally and has been known to swing on ropes off cliffs to alleviate boredom. Sam has written over 100 short stories and the novels 'Deadly Jewel' and 'The Eye of Shiva.' Both of these books are available on Amazon at http://www.amazon.com/Deadly-Jewel-Sam-Taylor-ebook/dp/B009F7K6SK

More Information

More information on upcoming volumes of Tales from the Perseus Arm, links to the authors' websites, Sam's Facebook and Twitter links, and information about SGA's other publications and services for authors, can be found at:

www.sgapublications.com